I0450830

Ray Bradbury sent a snail-mail fan letter
praising The Christmas Clock by John T. Cullen: "Bravo, John.
Loved your Clock!"—Ray Bradbury, January 2009

Clocktower Books

The Christmas Clock

by

John T. Cullen

The Christmas Clock

By John T. Cullen

Copyright © 2004 by John T. Cullen. All rights reserved.

This book has been released by Clocktower Books in print and digital editions. Check for e-book editions at major online retail sites, and print book editions at Amazon.com on line, or order a print copy in your local bookstore.

This novel is a work of historical fiction. Names, characters, places, and incidents are products of the author's imagination. Any resemblance to actual events or locales or persons, living or dead, is entirely coincidental.

www.clocktowerbooks.com/

Clocktower Books
6549 Mission Gorge Road, PMB 260
San Diego, California 92120

publishers@cox.net

All content, trademarks, tradenames, and other distinguishing marks, plus the cover art and cover text, are the intellectual property of John T. Cullen. Cover art and design by John T. Cullen.

Contents

Introducing Mr. Latchloose

The hero of our story, during this Christmas Season, was an older gentleman named Mr. Arthur Latchloose. He was quite wealthy—a banker, to be precise—and he had one remarkable hobby: collecting the very rarest of antiquarian treasures.

Mr. Arthur Latchloose had lived a full and interesting life, earning his college degree in Finance, serving in the Army as an officer, and then making a very successful career in banking. As a young man, he married his high school sweetheart right out of college, before he went off to war. When he returned, luckily in one piece and with a whole bunch of medals, he and Gretchen Latchloose got busy. They had two wonderful children, Eddie and Katie, who brought their parents all the usual happiness and heart-aches. Then, however, things got complicated and didn't go so well. There was a whole lot of heart ache and estrangement, and finally Gretchen passed away.

Arthur Latchloose was never the same after she died. He was a handsome older man, with a full head of white hair and a craggy face, and blue eyes that sparkled when he felt chatty—but that was not very often anymore. The kids moved away and didn't call or write, and Arthur couldn't figure out why.

Thus, Arthur was left alone, owning a drafty old bank building and a bunch of wonderful memories that faded a bit like the old photographs he kept all around his office. Try as he might, he couldn't help becoming a little bitter, and then a bit more bitter, and finally an old grouch. In the end, he kept to himself and puttered about his money and his antiquities. That was where his newest adventure in life began—when he acquired a remarkable grandfather clock originally made at the court of Louis XIV, the Sun King, for an Ottoman Sultan in Istanbul. By the time the Ottoman Empire became history after World War I, the clock had long since become the property of an Arab prince living near Baghdad, and finally, through some shenanigans, wound up in the possession of one Major Jarlid, late of the U.S. Army, now retired and alas not long for this world.

Jarlid needed money, and he found just the buyer for his priceless antiquity. You guessed it—Arthur Latchloose. Mr. Latchloose, however, had no idea about the danger and the potency of the mechanical wonder he was about to acquire.

Meanwhile, Christmas Season is a special time for writers and readers alike. Stories told during this period require a bit of extra sparkle and shine, a real warm-up that sets the proper mood. The opening chapter, therefore, dear reader, is devoted primarily to getting us in just the right mood. Christmas stories are different in that they hang upon not only the usual story elements—mystery, danger, and a bit of sheer fright, all of which exist within the caverns of this tale—but also hang upon a bit of the old, well, the old blarney if this author may say so. But this isn't just ordinary blarney, as you will soon find out. This story is about the strangest things that ever happened to Arthur Latchloose, and it may turn out to be the same for you.

Mood: A Snowy Evening in the City

One night right after the turn of the century—in a city we shall not name, at a time just before Christmas—snow fell silently on the rooftops, and the very air smelled of snow. The white crystals were dry and thick, and plummeted from an ash-colored sky.

A custard-bright moon with a shocked face floated behind drifting ships of cloud. Moonlight glittered on the river, under the bridges, on the frozen streets.

The snow flakes disappeared among the black zags and zigs of the skyline. Christmas angels in the sky blew icy polar winds that froze the distant rail lines, and iced up ships in the harbors, but warmed the human heart—if the person was in the right state of grace.

Falling, drifting snowflakes would vanish in the black-and-blue of a high, starry night sky. They silently and briefly reappeared in gritty circles of lantern glow on street corners. More and more flakes fell as the storm intensified. The flakes plummeted into rapidly accumulating flows and drifts along darkened house walls.

Snow muffled the slam of a door, a shout for a cab, a laugh at a joke, a goodnight, and a gunning motor. The air smelled briefly of exhaust. Gloomy pines in the park sighed in the wind, and their clean scent brushed the air clean.

Night and snow rimmed the glow of a clock's blue neon edge in a hairdresser's shop. Darkness framed a yellow beer sign in the corner of a tavern window. Dark light glittered on high-tech stainless steel lettering—on a shop selling fancy glass and steel coffee machines that were colored bright yellow or red or green or blue or just plain glossy white. One by one, shop lights winked out and doors rattled, as departing employees locked them. Each was on his or her way to a warm Christmas dinner by a tree full of ornaments and presents—even the few remaining, elderly employees of Latchloose Savings & Loan—all but Latchloose himself. He sat immobile, like a pale and horrid statue behind his great wooden desk, and heard people's footsteps that were muffled on the white sidewalks below his offices.

The streets were nearly empty, with a few last cars going here, and a few last pedestrians hurrying there. It was too late for the buses, and too early for the city plowing trucks. Here a Christmas wreath hung on a door, and there a string of colored lights traced a window frame. Somewhere on a chilly porch in a poor part of town, a row of children's boots stood in a row, and a kitchen was alive with pots banging and parents talking while the house smelled of baking turkey, of macaroni and cheese, of spices and fruits, while children laughed by the fireplace.

Most of the big city office buildings dimmed down, except for the glow of corridor lights. Most offices were empty, except for cleaning crews who must venture out. The shopping center with its neon and bright windows emptied quickly. There was a traffic jam, but it thinned out. Silence and emptiness reigned as the night deepened. The train station had been jammed with rush hour traffic, but now stood closed and abandoned for the night. The clock over the concrete platform read 11:50, barely visible through the ice crystals gathering on the glass and wrapping around the black, wrought-iron arches. Oh yes, and a very slight, cold wind moaned lightly, and keened as it circled around in ghostly white swirls.

Latchloose Building

There was one older brick building at the edge of that dimly glowing downtown. The Latchloose Building's battered red walls were covered with a lacy filigree of snow dust, like white ivy crawling up to drink moonlight. The old office building's windows were so dark they look like shiny black marble reflecting the amber street lights. But there was one window filled with a faint green light, and a lone figure dimly visible at a corner computer screen. The elderly man working in the solitude of his office late at night was one Arthur Latchloose, banker and real estate financier, who was exceedingly rich in money and exceedingly poor in all else. There he was again in his office—long after the staff had left, like just about every other day of the year.

He barely noticed the monotonous clanging of three bells in a nearby clocktower on the quarter hour, so close that one could almost feel the *ga-wump, ga-wump* of the mighty steel works thundering in their sturdy lumber containments and coffers. He ignored the bells, having felt their distant throbbing on thousands of solitary evenings. Instead, he focused on the computer whose greenish glow illuminated, in a sepulchral manner, his aging but still craggily handsome features.

Mr. Arthur Latchloose had acquired a tidy fortune in banking and real estate, and lived an exemplary life as he saw it. He and his late wife Gretchen raised two children, prayed in the right manner, did all the good and proper things, donated to charity, and supported worthy causes. In recent years Mr. Latchloose had a series of heartbreaks—Gretchen died of cancer, his children grew up and moved away out of contact, and it seemed to him the world had passed him by. He had memories aplenty, wonderful ones, of Christmases and other holidays when the children were small and Gretchen was still young and beautiful, but it had long since faded like the leaves on an autumn tree. He didn't think of himself as bitter, but more like disappointed. Some would say he was just sad, others that he was depressed, others that he was just a cranky and self-centered old man.

Arthur Latchloose did have one joy in life besides counting his money. He had a hobby—collecting antiquities; not antiques, because those were just recent bric-a-brac, but really old and very valuable stuff. He had long since stopped sending or receiving Christmas cards, and he had not exchanged gifts in a number of years since his grown children had abandoned him. Every year, however, he rewarded himself with a fine present. This year was going to be the best, for an old Army acquaintance had just offered to sell him a rare and unique clock. Latchloose had been waiting all evening for the other man's call—so long that he'd forgotten he was waiting.

Telephone

As Arthur Latchloose sat in his office, working into the night, the phone rang.

Mr. Latchloose was a bit eccentric in matters like this. A phone was a phone, not a canary or a cricket or a radio, and it should behave like a phone. His telephone was a black rubber gadget that long ago rode up and down in an elevator of the Empire State Building, when that structure was still brand-new. Mr. Latchloose refused to own any gadget that didn't behave as it should—so he was eager to find proper pencils that scratched on paper, scissors that snipped when they cut string, and clocks that ticked the seconds and rang the hours as a proper clock should.

Yes, the phone rang —it didn't warble or chirp or play a song like the newer phones—it rang honest-to-goodness like one of the earliest models. Those old phones from his childhood did not really ring so much, as they made a shrill grinding sound that penetrated down halls and corridors, throwing echoes into every room. At odd moments, they rang bell-like and song-like. For the most part, however, such ancient telephones ground and grated and rattled, like silvery chains yanked back and forth among the skeleton hands of Anguish, Regret, Warning, and all the other Imps of Malaise, who hovered as shadows among shadows— totally unlike the angelic and beautiful souls that hovered above the skyline, whose lips were blue, and their breath like polar winds, but their eyes alight with hopes and dreams.

Now who could be calling at this late hour? Mr. Latchloose looked distractedly at the telephone that sat in a pool of lemon-yellow light beside his desk blotter. For a moment, he regarded the treasures on his desk, while contemplating whether he felt like communicating with anyone just now. The desk pad was of thick cowhide with thick, creamy blotter paper that had a few ink speckles—it once sat on the desk of a Seattle shipping king. The silver pen-and-pencil set bore the logo of an extinct airline that pioneered the skies of the 1930s. Ah yes, Major Jarlid. He'd almost forgotten. Latchloose lifted the receiver. "Yes?"

"Latchloose, do you have the money?" said a deep voice.

"Yes." Arthur brimmed with excitement, but he knew how to play it cool and drive a hard bargain. "Jarlid, I thought you'd gone sour on our deal."

"A deal is a deal," said the booming voice on the other end. He sounded like a man who forever spoke with his chin buried in his chest, and had black burning eyes to boot. "I've had my share of bad luck since I retired from the service, and this clock is my last item of value to trade in for the money I need."

Latchloose fought a quiver of interest, tempered with much residual suspicion. Then he calmed himself, remembering that he'd known Jarlid in the Army and he'd seemed like an upright fellow. Also, Latchloose had taken the precaution of visiting a Mr. Threadcarpet at the Antiquities Mongers Exchange, who had vouched for the integrity of Jarlid and the authenticity of his rare clock. "Very well, then, let's get to it. I have yet to see the clock, and then I'll debit your internet account."

"I'll be by in a few minutes to pick you up." The Major's voice had that commanding boom to it.

Latchloose blinked and leaned over to look out the window, which was rimed with frost. "Tonight? There is a snowstorm and—"

"Now or never, Latchloose."

"And the price remains fixed as we agreed?"

"Solid as a rock, and no tricks about it."

Arthur hemmed a little, hawed a bit, and then said: "Very well, I'll meet you outside. How long will you be?"

"I'm coming around the corner as we speak, in my car."

Major Jarlid

A rthur went through the same solitary, forlorn routine as every other day. He shut down his accounting program and turned off the computer. He put on his heavy, dark wool coat, gray felt Homburg, and paisley scarf. He picked up his black umbrella with the lacquered walnut handle, turned out the lights, and locked up his private fourth-floor office. The dark lumber and sagging bricks of his building had monkish smells— floor polish, dead candles, and endless tisking and head-shaking, where no child could find happiness, and no bright spirit wanted to tarry.

The hallway was cramped and musty, with bare brick walls visible by the light of a single sickly-weak, bare light bulb. Arthur peeked from an upper window and saw the long black limousine waiting by the curb. Its amber parking lights glowed under fresh snow, and exhaust came in a cloud from its tailpipe.

Arthur trudged down the narrow wooden stairs, past the third floor administrative offices, and down to the second floor bookkeeping department. The corridor here was a bit more modern, but still worn and plain with green linoleum floors and scratched aluminum doors. Arthur set alarms as he went. He owned the building, and it rustled familiarly around him. He strode through the marble-floored main lobby with its circle of dark mahogany teller cages. It was an old bank, and by day the tellers stood behind black iron bars topped with gilded scrollwork, as bank tellers should, so Arthur felt rather strongly. He resisted all entreaties to modernize, to expand, to make the staff more comfortable. Besides, all that cost money.

Outside, the snow had let up a bit. The wind had blown knee-deep drifts against the bank building. Now it whirled feather-like flakes about, which had landed on the drifts but not yet become part of them.

Arthur clutched his umbrella close with one elbow and hung on to his hat and scarf as he leaned into the wind.

A minute later, he was in the warmth of Jarlid's limousine. He peeled off his scarf in the dry heat. The two men shook hands. Jarlid's grip was still strong, but he looked jaundiced and emaciated. The once robust features were gaunt, the fiery eyes sunken and hollowed, the skin sallow and gray. Arthur didn't express his shock, but Jarlid had become a rack of bones, wearing a plaid green shirt and baggy jeans.

Jarlid grinned, showing large yellow teeth edged with gray. "I don't eat well these days. I'm afraid my stomach doesn't tolerate much any more. I contracted something strange in the distant wars. I was forced me to retire, and to seek what little help and hope I might find to live another year or two."

Arthur voiced concern as they prowled down streets blinded by snow whirling around street lamps. The occasional pedestrian disappeared here in a doorway, there into a car to go home for the holiday. Arthur had lost track of Jarlid, until an unexpected phone call a few days earlier. Jarlid had reintroduced himself after many years, and offered a fabulous clock. "In which war was it that you found this thing?"

"It was the Mesopotamian War."

"Oh, which one of the many?" Arthur asked.

"One of the more recent ones." Jarlid leaned forward and regarded Arthur with haunted eyes. "I was still in good health then, a vigorous man with a long future ahead. One night, I was driving from a town on the Tigris to a town on the Euphrates with a small infantry convoy. It was one of those moonlit nights when the desert seems to glow, and a chilly wind sweeps down from the north. We were attacked, and the two men I was riding with in an armored car tried to make a run across a field. A mine exploded, overturning the car, and the other two were killed. I managed to stagger to my feet. I fell repeatedly, which saved my hide. With gun in hand, I kept moving along. I could hear the enemy converging on the burning car behind me, and that drew their attention away while I crawled away through a muddy ditch. I continued on, running and staggering, until I fell down in a dead faint.

"When I awoke, people had carried me into a house. I lay in a bed. What a house it was, a small palace with all the latest conveniences, but it was a very old place. You could tell from the wear in the wooden paneling on the walls, and the mosaics in the floors that looked almost Roman, and statues with broken noses standing around bubbling fountains. I tell you, Latchloose, the very air smelled different, faintly fragrant like a spring garden, yet faintly musty as if it was pent up somehow a long time. The people here looked different than those I was used to seeing. They seemed concerned, but languid and without fear. Everyone else in the world has that dark, gnawing look of worry—especially people who don't speak proper English, and live in a land of perpetual war. These people seemed languid and self-assured. I grasped that they had rescued me, taken me into their estate, and that I was quite safe. I learned all this as they moved around me—yet nobody spoke, at least not a language I could understand. I think they spoke mind-to-mind, telepathically, as if they were exchanging warm blood among each other as one organism. It was quite strange, even for that region, to be sure.

"I wasn't badly injured and mended quickly, but I felt very weak and slept a lot for some undetermined time. I spent most of the while in a small apartment unit overlooking palm trees and a river in quite a lush garden. As soon as I felt a bit better, I demanded to leave, so I could return to my unit. Finally, a tiny little dark-haired woman appeared in the doorway and beckoned me to follow her. She wore an intricately designed silk dress much like a mustard-green Indian sari, with many delicate little flowers printed into its folds. She brought me to a garden in which sat a very odd man upon a large burgundy pillow with tassels on each corner. He was dressed somewhat like a pasha of the old Turkish regime, with a red fez wrapped in a turban. He was wrapped in a robe and had a broad sword by his side in a lavishly embroidered leather and linen sheath. *My guest,* he boomed at me in our own language, as plainly as I speak with you now, only his words flowed silently around me, throbbing softly in my ears like the beating of my own heart. *My guest, you are feeling well enough to leave?*

"I thanked him for his hospitality and told him I was indeed ready to rejoin my unit. To that he replied, *We will gladly do for you what else we can—we have already done more than you know.* For that I thanked him, and asked what I might do in return. He shook his head and took me down a long, dark hallway into the bowels of his palace. What a place this was! No Western person would ever live this way. The floors were of marble polished to a high luster, inset with marginal mosaic patterns in semiprecious stones. Silk and brocade draperies hung down, too long for the walls, and piled in stiff folds on the floors. The halls were carpeted with the finest Oriental rugs, sometimes four or five deep. In wall niches stood statues of all kinds, from mythological heroes and writhing cherubs to beautiful goddesses like Diana with her bow and arrows, and her wild animals that tore men to pieces if they glimpsed her swimming naked in a forest pond."

At that, Arthur laughed. "You must have been hallucinating!"

"Maybe, Latchloose, maybe; who knows? I had been injured and sick, and who knows what drugs they poured into me to help me mend? I glimpsed a room with pillars surrounding a pool steaming with perfume and littered with flowers, in which pale nymphs laughed and splashed each other. The air had an odd, incense-like tinge, and I saw flickering candle-flames in wall sconces shaped like seashells. The whole thing was like a dream, I tell you. The pasha descended from his dais. The old woman led me from one hall to the next, past separate rooms, in which handsome young men sang softly, and others in which shrouded young women played all manner of exotic instruments. In the pasha's company, we came to a single room in which stood only one thing—a very ornate clock."

"A clock?" Arthur said. "Our clock?" At last the major seemed to broach the object of this trip in the middle of the night during a winter storm. They passed through intersections, past billboards, past darkened buildings, as Jarlid drove with a slow and steady hand. Now he fumbled in a trouser pocket and pulled out a shiny object.

"Yes, our clock, and also this watch," said Major Jarlid. He pressed into Arthur's hands a large vest pocket watch, of the kind worn long ago by train conductors, and earlier by men like Benjamin Franklin. It felt cool to the touch, and Arthur weighed it idly from one hand to the other. It was moderately heavy, and finely tooled in beaten silver and brass with elaborate, well-worn scrollwork. For a moment, he felt blood rushing in his ears. Arthur flicked the watch open. He gazed upon an antique watch dial, with black Roman numerals on a brown-pitted, creamy surface like mottled parchment, under thick glass.

"That," said Major Jarlid "is the heart of the thing. There I was, in the company of this strange pasha, and the old woman, in an empty room with fine oak floor boards and simple wall paper in a delicate design of tiny flowers, not unlike her sari I just described. We walked up to the clock and we each tapped a fingertip on its broad base. It sounded hollow, but echoes careened from wall to wall inside. It was intricately made, with many fine touches.

"That's when he told me it was made at the Court of the Sun King in France, Louis XIV, in the Year 1710 Anno Domini. Of course they didn't call them grandfather clocks then, but floor clocks or long-case clocks."

Latchloose nodded. He too knew this story. An American composer, Henry Work, in 1875, had written a little ditty called *The Grandfather Clock*. Work was staying at the George Hotel in Piercebridge, North Yorkshire, England, which had a remarkable—and dead—floor clock. It was some seven feet tall, as was customary, because of the required pendulum length, and the drop need of its weights. As the weights slowly dropped, the mechanism unwound, so to speak; raising the weights back up reset such a clock. Two very aged brothers named Jenkins owned the hotel, and their clock was renowned for its accuracy. When one of the brothers died, the clock seemed, however, to become sick, eventually losing up to an hour a day. No clockmaker—and plenty came to the challenge—was ever able to fix it, and the clock totally froze the minute the surviving Jenkins brother died, 90 years old. Like that, the clock sat in the hotel lobby for many years—the world's first grandfather clock. But enough of such digressions.

"So there it was," Jarlid said of his own clock that he was selling to Arthur. "What a beauty. Made by an English clockmaker in Paris, and remade in some Turkish *atelier* with Moorish and Saracen touches. The craftsmen perfected it with Ottoman flowers of delicate soapstone mosaic, mother of pearl, and carved scrolls in sandalwood and other fine woods, inlaid and lacquered, so that it made one dizzy to look into its many facets and faces.

"That strange little pasha said to me, *This clock will buy you the time you need. Touch it, and move on to the rest of your life.* The old woman held open a door, showing me a tranquil desert outside, while the pasha made waving motions for me to get out of there. I was torn by conflicting emotions—part of me wanted to stay, and sink deeper into the timeless ennui of that peaceful oasis, while the other part of me longed to escape back to fresh air, sunshine, and wonderful life.

"I stopped in my conflict and anguish, in the midst of that marbled monument, that tomb of minutes and hours, that gilded and mosaic shrine of pillars and domed ceiling, and boomed at them: *Who are you anyway? Why do you care about me, and how do you know where I am going?* I shuddered at the sound of my own voice, which shuddered like the drowning bell of a sinking ship.

"But the pasha and the old woman had disappeared. I heard wind sighing in the desert outside. Somewhere, distant artillery boomed in the never-ending wars over Armageddon's horizons. I stood alone, looking up into a lapis-lazuli dome, where the gilded twelve tokens of the Zodiac shimmered in gray shadow. For a moment, I inhaled a cosmic connection, which interlaced the twelve hours of day, and the twelve hours of night, with the twelve months of the astrological year (which was invented not far from that place, by spirits still hovering in the sands). For a moment, I thought I saw huge hands sweeping around, past the Waterman, past the Virgin, past the Scorpion, past the Twins, and the other gilded symbols of time.

"I hesitated, while wind kicked up across the marble tiles, and threw sand and grit around the feet of that marvelous clock. On impulse, I lifted the clock—it was light as a feather, despite its weight and wooden hull riveted with steel like a ship's hull. It only took me a few seconds to carry it on my back, out into the desert, while the doorway to that magical place closed behind me."

"You stole it?" Latchloose said with a gasp. "What if it is cursed? What if it kills me? Look, you are already half dead…" Latchloose grabbed Jarlid's wrist and squeezed his thumb against the joint—but it felt warm to the touch. A pulse ticked away in slow beats, one every second.

Jarlid's eyes were black, blazing coals. "I prefer to think of myself as half alive if anything!" He yanked his hand away with annoyance. "You certainly think of nobody but yourself."

"Very well," said Latchloose. He reached into his pocket and pulled out a plastic freezer bag, the size of a sandwich baggie, but of a far thicker mil rating. Inside was a stack of hundred dollar bills circled by several stout rubber bands Arthur had found in his bank's supplies closet. "Here is the money, if you'll be so kind as to take me to my clock."

Jarlid drove on through the blinding snow. Thick flakes flew like fists toward the windshield. The wipers thumped back and forth. The heater sighed, faintly smelling of hot water, antifreeze, and machine oil. "I have to tell you the last little bit."

"There's more?" Arthur asked suspiciously.

"Yes, I have no choice. You see, there I was in the middle of the night, lugging this clock through the desert. The oasis from which I had just emerged was gone—vanished under the dunes and starlight. The clock was strangely light, as if it wanted me to carry it. I had no idea where I was going. The sky was so black, and so filled with stars, that I could not recognize any constellations to navigate by. Then, I heard a voice. *Jarlid*, a man's voice addressed me quite clearly.

"I stopped and looked around. I put the clock down and wiped my brow. It was cold and dry, and there was a little piercing wind, but my sweat was more from guilt and fear at having stolen this clock. *Jarlid*, said a shadowy figure standing on a nearby drift of sand. I could tell it was a young man in a suit, like a New York stock broker, with short hair, no beard, and quite a nice pleasant Midwestern American accent (or the lack of an accent, therewith). I managed to say *Who are you?* But he stepped down beside me in a nonce, almost as if he'd shape-shifted in an instant, from one place to the other. He said: *You have to sign for the clock.*

"I must have guffawed, however one does that. I scoffed. *What do you mean, sign for it?* I had stolen it, and I thought he meant I must give it back. I already regretted my impulsive crime.

"*Right over here*, said he. Lo and behold, the air around us shimmered as if we were inside a chapel, or a bank. *That's right, on your left a bit.* He waved his hand for me to follow the direction of his gesture. I walked to a marble table, which was embedded in a sand dune under an oddly amber and runny light, as if it were flowing liquid. The counter top was black, with white veins, and felt cool to the touch, so real did it seem. On its surface lay a kind of heavy ledger, with a contract of some sort clipped inside its gutter. *Go on,* he said, *sign so we can get on with our business.* He pointed to a gilded pen stuck in a holder, and an inkwell with an ornate golden lid. I lifted out the pen, dipped it in the inkwell, and scratched my name on the parchment. He nodded approvingly, slammed the book shut, and stuck it under his arm. *Thank you. Well done.*

"So now what? I asked. You take your clock back and I get to go home, is that it?

"No quite. He grinned and stood with his fists on his hips. Haven't you guessed? I am the djinni of this place. My poor owner was stuck with this thing until you took it. He was a thousand years old, and has seen more armies moving among these dunes, more kings and generals at war with each other, and more lost souls wandering under the stars—but he has gone to his reward now, a free man.

"Take your wretched clock, I said. If that's the case, I want no part of it.

"He, however, said: You took it, you've signed for it, and the clock is now yours. Your fate and its fate are entwined. I am of the djinni who saved you when you lay dying at the edge of our twilight realm. Don't be afraid, we have no intention of harming you.

"He then reached up into the silvered and ornately scrolled, shining clock face, twisted a lever, and from the center of its long case, he pulled off this watch I have given you to hold. He said: *This clock can bring you either great joy or great sorrow. You have a pact with it, which you must honor to the last jot and the last tittle.*

"*How do I do that?* I asked the djinni," said Jarlid.

The djinni pointed to that vest pocket clock I still held, and said, This is the heart of the thing, that which beats and makes the time flow through its veins the way blood flows through yours, and the way magic desert sand flows through mine. Through his watch, the great clock gives you time enough to do what you must. When your time was just about over, you must pass it along to the next deserving soul, and then his time will be extended just as yours has been. But there is one thing: You are obliged to be totally honest with the next owner, as I have been with you. You must be honest, and always seek truth.

Arthur looked dubiously at the watch. "You mean I could still give this back and cancel our deal?"

Jarlid shook his head. "That's not how it works. Once you have coveted this watch, and the great clock whose heart it is, she is yours for as long as there is not the next person who covets her.

"That could be forever!" Latchloose shrieked. "What am I getting into?"

Jarlid grinned. "Something wonderful, my friend. Have no fear. If at heart you are a just and honest man, the clock will beat for you. If you are not, it will beat against you—it will beat you, no matter how clever you think you are. You have to go with its program."

"Do I still have a choice?" Arthur wanted the clock, which was ornate and beautiful—he'd seen pictures on line—but he wasn't so sure anymore.

"Do you know, Latchloose, I have no idea what I said next. Perhaps I fainted. The last I saw of him was his grin and the strange, hard glitter of his very black eyes. I could swear—he seemed to just sort of dissolve into a million golden slivers of light that slowly faded in midair.

"When I came to my senses, I lay in a military hospital bed near Baghdad, on a sunny day with a nice breeze coming in the window and the sounds of traffic and then of course the ever-haunting river of prayer that flows from the minarets and mosques in a flood of praise to Allah. That sound of the muezzin at prayer stays in the mind. It flows like traffic and wraps itself around one's heart and soul. Have you ever been there, Latchloose?"

Arthur admitted he had not. "I have seen it on the evening news," he allowed. "I was lucky enough to serve my Army days in a warm, cozy office looking out the window whenever the urge pressed me. I have been to Rome and Paris and London, mainly to buy old things. I wanted to visit Egypt and Mesopotamia, but those places always seem so far and dangerous."

"Ah yes," the major said in a faint, weak voice. "Nobody who has been there comes back the same as he went." He pointed to the watch in Arthur's hand. "Keep that in your pocket at all times." He added: "I am dying. I need cash very badly to fly across country to be with family, and I have no possible further use for the clock or that watch. All I need from you was five grand, and it's all yours."

"Very well then," Arthur said. "I'm in the game. Like yourself, I have nothing to lose." On the cautious note, he entertained second thoughts of waiting. Maybe he should hire an escrow company, as with any other major purchase. The escrow served as middleman (or middlewoman), a neutral party holding the seller's goods, and the buyer's money, until the transfer could be completed in a fair, safe, and orderly manner.

Jarlid said: "The clock has chosen its next owner well. I am just the messenger."

They drove along the snowy streets in silence, and the city fell behind them as they crept into the suburbs at the edge of town.

Escrow Didn't Happen

H ere we are," Major Jarlid finally said. He parked under a towering billboard advertising Rose Attar's Grand Self-Storage. There, they stepped from the car and bundled their collars against the cold. Arthur looked up at the glittering sign whose frame was filled with snow. His breath escaped in ragged wisps. Jarlid, meanwhile, entered the well-lit office to get a key at the service desk.

Arthur trudged after Jarlid, to a storage unit far back amid snowy hills and pine forests under moonlight. Without knowing how he knew, Arthur knew what that building was. It was a time storage. It was a building that stood alone, shrouded in night, with nary a light inside. It was one of those buildings whose insides changed every time you came to it. One time your unit was on the ground floor, and the next time it was far away through a rabbit-warren of dusty wooden stairways. Nothing ever stayed the same, just as time flowed ever onward, like a river whose waters never pass any place more or less than once.

They stood before a simple rollup door overlooking a side driveway. Jarlid opened the padlock with a rattle of chains and key, and lifted the rolling gate. There, wrapped in blankets, stood a tall object, glittering in diffuse light from stars and snow outside. Jarlid walked around it, pulling the covers off.

"It certainly is beautiful," Arthur said, breathlessly, as they stood looking at the magnificent Louis XIV clock. In his right hand, in the warmth of his pocket, he tightly held the trainman's watch Major Jarlid sold him. Arthur started to forget his doubts. He was excited by the night's adventure and looking taking home his greater acquisition.

"I'll need the money right now," Jarlid said. He gripped Arthur's upper arm in a vise-like grip. "I have no more time to waste on idle conversation. My time is running out."

"Ouch! I beg your pardon." Arthur was stunned. He'd had visions of calling an escrow firm the next day to arrange a proper, supervised exchange. The clock would stand on a carpeted floor, and Arthur would sit with his check book at a table right next to it, and Jarlid opposite Arthur at the table. Jarlid would have to wait a bit in his impatience. He shook Jarlid's iron grip away.

Jarlid, however, was insistent. He stepped directly in front of Arthur and regarded him with large, hypnotic eyes. "My dear Latchloose," said Major Jarlid, "you will write me a check, and you will do so right now. Then I will disappear from your life, and you will forget all about me. You will be busy with a whole new range of things you had not imagined."

"I will do no such thing," Arthur said, weakening.

"You have become a cranky, selfish old man," Jarlid said. His eyes bored into Arthur's soul like glowing red-hot embers. "You had a beautiful wife, and you ignored her in your rise to the top of the financial pyramid. You had two beautiful if not exactly perfect offspring, and you live alienated from them. Those are your problems, Latchloose. I have too many problems of my own to worry about yours. This I can promise you, however. With this clock you are buying, you won't be able to run from your own miserable selfishness much longer. You will have to be honest with yourself and others. Time would have it no other way."

"I—" Arthur started to say, and no more words came out of his mouth, so he snapped it shut. Instead, in a dreamy state, as if he were moving slowly in molasses, he took out his plastic bag of bills, and handed it to Major Jarlid.

Jarlid scribbled out a receipt, using a stubby pencil on a piece of cardboard torn from a dusty box. Without a word of thanks, Major Jarlid handed the shred of cardboard to Arthur. Jarlid turned and vanished amid a whirl of snowflakes. Arthur looked on in stunned silence, and when he snapped his mouth shut, he had forgotten all about Major Jarlid. He was, however, filled with anticipation at taking home his new grandfather clock—to his office, that is, to gloat over it, alone and in the dark.

To keep the magnificent clock safe, he rattled down the door, slammed it shut, clicked the lock in place, and carried the key back to the office. The heavy silver watch throbbed in Arthur's hand inside his coat pocket.

Already, the tire tracks of Major Jarlid's car had almost entirely disappeared under wispy new snow. The city skyline glowed, a haze of stained-glass and neon, just visible through a cleft in some dark hills. It seemed as if angels were singing with frosty voices under the stars and above the falling snow.

The First Hour

Pushing the door open, Arthur entered the all-night clerk's office. A middle-aged woman sat at a desk, reading a newspaper in the greenish glow of a library lamp. "Can I help you?"

"I came to pick something up." Arthur stamped snow from his shoes and walked up to the counter. He laid his business card down on the worn brown countertop. He put the key down next to it, but the key vanished as if he'd never had it.

"The units are locked for the night," she said, rising and walking toward him with her arms folded together over her bosom, under a thick woolen shawl. "What a night to be out. Are you having some kind of emergency?"

Arthur didn't know quite what to say, and somehow he knew he didn't need to say much. He pushed the card forward a few inches with his fingertips.

She started to say: "Can't help you at this hour, Mister." She saw the card and fell silent . She looked at him, at the card, and at him again with a light of realization dawning on her features. "You are—?"

"Arthur Latchloose."

She nodded. "Ah yes." She extended a soft, heavy hand. "I'm Rose Attar. You can call me Rose." She was a fiftyish woman, slightly fuller and squarer than one might expect, and there was gray around the roots of her dyed-blond hair, but her features were pleasant, handsome, and symmetrical, with an angular jaw and full mouth, and sympathetic blue eyes. "Okay," she said dreamily, "I get it. You came for the clock."

"You knew about it then?"

She seemed momentarily confused. "Yes. I don't know how or why, but I knew you were coming. I'll get the night man to bring it around." She picked up a desk phone, dialed, and waited.

Arthur heard a distant ringing on the other end of the line. She cupped her hand over the mouthpiece and whispered: "I'm surprised you'd be here—or anyone working with you—at this hour, in the storm."

"I want my clock very badly, and I can pay extra for quick service getting it home," Arthur said.

"We'll see what we can do," she said. Arthur heard a man's voice on the other end, from across the counter. She turned away and muttered instructions. Hanging up, she told Arthur: "The night man will be right over."

"That will be great." Arthur felt the watch in his hand, in his pocket. The watch felt warm and alive, almost like a beating heart that wanted to be reunited with its body. For a moment, he thought it wriggled like a fish. Or maybe his hand had simply twitched for no reason.

The door opened, and a man stomped in, brushing snow off his clothes. He was a thin, tall, graying man who looked as if he had been an athlete long ago. His mouth and chin had a crisp look, with small evenly set teeth, to match a hawkish nose and cutting eyes. "This the gentleman?"

"Yes, this is Mr. Latchloose." To Arthur, she introduced the newcomer as Roger Cup handle.

Cup handle extended a hard, vise-like hand. "I'm the night man here, and I do everything. Rose tells me you have a clock you want to pick up from storage with us."

"If you don't mind." There was something odd about Cup handle, and Arthur couldn't quite put his finger on it. Maybe his eyes looked just a trifle shifty. Arthur was a pretty decent judge of people, and he had a nagging doubt about his fellow.

"Come on." He turned and led Arthur out into the wintry landscape, while Rose stayed leaning against the counter inside with her arms again folded under the shawl.

It was a short ride among the white-dusted lanes among the storage units. "You get ready for Christmas?" Cup handle said by way of making conversation.

"I'm afraid it's been some years since I bothered."

"Now that doesn't seem so reasonable."

Arthur examined the inventory of his losses. "I just don't have any reason to."

"Reason is only the half of it. The other half is fun, faith, frivolity. Think about how crazy you have to be to fall in love and get married. I'm sure you were at that point once."

"Long ago. My wife has died, and my children have moved away." He wished Cup handle would be quiet and mind his own business.

"Children move away far?" Cup handle seemed entirely at ease in the warmth of the cab, and Arthur was grateful the truck was so new and clean.

"Far enough. We've lost contact."

"Now how was that? I've got family all over the country, and we manage to at least call each other, if not visit. If you don't mind me asking. Sounds like there's some bad blood there, Mister."

"I wouldn't go that far. My wife and I, we had a wonderful life together, until she got sick and faded away. Cancer, you know."

"I'm sorry to hear."

"Thanks. Yes, it's never been the same since. And then my son and daughter, well, they went their separate ways and we all seem to have lost interest in each other. Well, to tell the truth, I was disappointed that…" Arthur stopped talking because the other man wouldn't understand, and on the surface maybe it sounded selfish, but he had wanted Edward to take over the business from him, and Anne not to marry a failure like this Tim Wood pond she'd dredged up at some church social, instead of a successful lawyer or banker. Not only had Gretchen betrayed him, by going off and dying like that, but his children had turned against him. He finished lamely: "It's a chicken and egg thing, you know? Who knew who struck the first blow or said the first hurtful words. It just went spinning out of control."

Cup handle leaned a little bit into a corner as the truck slipped on ice and then corrected. "Yes, that's how it goes. Nobody wants to say they're sorry, or admit they might have been wrong. Even a little bit. Nobody wants to open the door a crack."

"Aren't those the same thing, saying sorry and admitting you've been wrong?" Arthur knew he had not been wrong. Neither had anyone else. The good life and its prospects had just slipped away.

Cup handle grinned. "Why quibble? You can say you're sorry without admitting you might have been wrong. You have to learn to be more irrational. Go with the flow, as they say. Maybe a person is sorry because they feel bad. That's not the same as saying they were wrong. Suddenly everyone feels good again, and we don't have to know why. That's how it's done—you just do it."

Arthur tired of the conversation and didn't answer. It opened too many old wounds, and didn't solve anything. He had not spoken with his children Eddie and Katie (or their spouses and children) in more years than that. It seemed like an eternity…an eternity since the days of those smiling family portraits, the little kids, the innocence, the hopes, the family trips. Come to think of it, he'd never actually planned any of it. Gretchen had always organized all those things, be it the trip to the Grand Canyon, or a trip to the photographer's for a family portrait. Arthur had always been too busy at the bank to think of those things. He still really missed Gretchen , though that last sorrow-filled year of her dying from leukemia was over a decade ago.

"Here we are," Cup handle said, and Arthur was grateful for the break in his dreary thoughts. They got out and Cup handle punched in a number code on a pad beside a door, and then they were in the dry, temperature-controlled storage building. The stairs were unfinished plywood, the walls unfinished drywall. It was all as utilitarian and spare as could be. Cuphandle said: "Here's your unit."

"So how long has this clock sat here?" Arthur asked as the door swung open.

"Way longer than I've been here, and that's about two years." As he spoke, Cuphandle seemed to grow larger somehow, or was it his shadow thrown on the rough wall behind him by the hallway light? The closer he stood to the clock, the stronger his beard shadow, the bigger his forehead, and the higher his collar stood up around his ears. At first, Arthur didn't quite notice these apparent changes much.

There the clock was: every bit as lovely and complex as Major Jarlid had said. The clock was feminine, with a full bottom and a narrow waist and a tapering top. Its clock face shimmered like an engraving with a thousand fine lines whirling in fingerprint complexity. Its numbers were Roman, large, stark, and black. Every available corner, surface, and edge was decorated with the finest carvings on marble and wood and metal surfaces. It gleamed, and seemed to call Arthur to it.

"Do you have the vest pocket watch?" Cuphandle asked.

"The what?" As Arthur regarded him, he noticed that the man seemed to have changed. Startled, Arthur pulled out the stop watch. "You mean this?"

"Yes." Cuphandle grinned and rubbed his hands together. "So you signed the contract, I take it, and the clock is yours?"

"Yes," Arthur said almost breathlessly. He hardly noticed the other man's excited breathing, flushed cheeks, and gleaming eyes. The trainman's watch burned in his palm as he took it out and held it up to the grandfather (grandmother?) clock. The clock almost pulled his eyes toward it, and there, just under the round clock face, was a depression shaped just like the watch.

"Go on," Cuphandle urged. "You have to do this yourself. Go on, listen to your heart. The clock is telling you what to do."

In modern, digitoid parlance, this was a kind of docking station for the watch. Without debating, Arthur held up the watch and moved it close to the concavity. The watch fit in, was almost sucked in, with the satisfying click of an expensive car door whispering shut. Levers and ratchets ground powerfully as the clock pulled its heart close, its child, its nestling. In that moment, something came over the clock and indeed over the entire room. Arthur half expected the clock to begin booming out the hours. Instead, a change happened in the clock face. He saw now what it was: He'd seen only the hour and minute hands, typical of clocks of its era. Now it seemed the clock face became animated in greater detail. A second-hand began ticking around the circle, and the clock's tocking grew in intensity. Arthur wondered who had kept it wound all this time. Did it have an atomic engine of some sort? Had alchemists at the court of the Sun King, or at the divan of the Sultan, contrived to stoke this grand clock with a smidgin of the sun's almost inexhaustible power? Did the fire of the sun and the gravity of the moon somehow keep its esoteric engines grinding in refined synchronicity?

"The energy of Time itself," Cuphandle whispered. He seemed to have grown until he was eight feet tall. His upper arms had grown massive, rippling with muscles as he folded them across his chest. His clothing had changed, also, to something resembling a hybrid between a khaki flight suit and Turkish dress with pantaloons and puffy blouse. "Do you know who I am?" he boomed at Arthur.

Arthur shook his head. Oddly, he didn't feel afraid. He had that same groggy feeling he got when awakening in the middle of the night to stagger down a dim corridor for a glass of water, then returning to sleep in his bed without ever having fully awakened.

"I come with the clock," Cuphandle said. "I am the djinni of the clock."

"The what?"

"Genie, you know, like found in a bottle? It's an English word, from the Arabic djinni, from the ancient Roman genius, whose plural in Latin was genii."

Arthur was surprised. "You mean, like the genie Aladdin found in the sand in a bottle?"

Cuphandle nodded. "Yes, near the sea. The sea of time, I might add."

"You don't say."

Cuphandle looked down over crossed, muscular arms. "When you bought the clock, you got a piece of me too."

Arthur stood with his mouth hanging open, and could only manage to say "What?"

"You probably thought djinn only live in jars, stuck there until someone lets them out. Djinn is plural in Arabic, for two or more djinni-guys. Actually, virtually every place and thing has its djinni. It's just that some djinn are smarter than others, and I'm one of the smartest."

Arthur put his hands on his hips. "This is all so utterly ridiculous, Mr. Cuphandle. Have you been drinking?"

Cuphandle raised his hands in a 'search me' gesture. "Not a drop, Mr. Latchloose." Now it was Cuphandle's turn to put his hands on his hips. "See here, Latchloose, you've got limited time and you don't want to waste any of it, so start believing in me and let's not waste a lot of time arguing about your doubts."

Arthur kept his hands on his hips, and the two glared at each other thus. Arthur said: "I want you to either haul this thing to my home, or get someone up here who will do it for me, and stop talking drivel."

"Very well," said Cuphandle. Wrapping his enormous arms around the clock, he lifted it easily as if it were a light thing filled with air. He carried it out the door in a few easy steps.

"Easy! Careful!" Arthur cried out, hopping after him, down the corridor, to the stairs.

"Not to worry. Oh, do close the door and turn off the lights behind us, would you? Let's not waste energy."

Grumbling, Arthur did as he was told. By the time he pulled the outside door shut with a loud click, and joined Cuphandle by the truck, Cuphandle already had the clock wrapped in quilts, safely covered with a heavy black tarp, and strapped down with thick blue and white nylon cords.

"Where to, boss?" asked Cuphandle.

Arthur told him his address—reluctantly—adding, "You don't plan to stay there with the clock, I hope."

As they sat in the warm cab again, and Cuphandle drove bouncing over the speed bumps, Cuphandle said: "Not to worry; I have her strapped in and wrapped as delicately as eggs. In regard to my domicile, I do indeed stay with the clock—"

"Oh no!" Arthur protested loudly and angrily.

"—At least for the first twelve hours," Cuphandle finished his sentence. "You see, unlike those djinn in bottles, we clock types only award you one wish, and you have to make it, and we must fulfill it, in exactly twelve hours from the time you signed the purchase from the previous owner. He didn't explain all this to you, did he?"

Arthur shook his head. "I don't recall off-hand from whom I bought it, come to think." He raised his palms to his temples, and violently shook his head, but no memory came. The immediate past was partially a muddled blank.

"No matter," Cuphandle said. He tapped the large round clock face in his truck's dashboard. "In fact, your first hour is almost up, so you only have eleven hours left. What is it that you desire most in life?"

Arthur laughed. "Assuming I believe all this poppycock?"

"What have you got to lose?"

"That's true," Arthur said. "Okay, suppose I play along with your silly game. What is it I want most of all? Do I have to be careful what I say? Like if I wish I had another million bucks, will you drop a zillion pounds of reindeer on my head?"

"No, no, nothing like that," said Cuphandle. "That's for those dorky lamp djinni that one occasionally finds washed up on a beach. They play nasty little games like that. I'm a professional, and take pride in delivering quality service with that fawning, customer-is-always right smile, and of course your happiness with the outcome is the key." He added rather darkly: "Even if I want to strangle you at times. And you do seem like a prime strangling magnet."

Arthur thought a bit. "You know, if I had at least two wishes, maybe the first one would be that you tell me nothing but the truth."

Cuphandle shrugged. "True, but a lamp djinni would figure out some way to play with the words and lie to you. You'll just have to trust my honesty. Truthfulness is built into the clock and all that it touches. Time is truth, and time does not lie. I urge you, however, to consider your choice very carefully, because you truly will be stuck with it forever."

"Oh come on. This is just a game, right?"

Cuphandle grew a bit huffy. "Listen, you old fool who believes in nothing, and cares only about himself. Don't anger me or I'll change you into a dog and leave you at someone's doorstep. Then your only wish would be to change back into your miserable self."

"That would defeat your customer service philosophy," Arthur said with malevolent sarcasm.

"True. Okay, let's try this. See that tree over there?" Cuphandle pulled over on the narrow two-lane road, and pointed to a snow-covered tree. "I want you to point at that tree and say *Poof*, got that?"

"You must think I am as nuts as you are," Arthur said. He kept his hands firmly, palms-down, on the seat on either side of him.

"Let me show you," Cuphandle said. He pointed at the tree and said "*Poof.*" Instantly, all the snow disappeared from the tree's barren, black, icy branches, and it stood fully resplendant with a full crown of midsummer leaves bursting from every branch, stem, and twig."

Arthur stared in disbelief. "Holy Mackerel. I must be dreaming."

Cuphandle seemed unperturbed, as if he did this sort of thing routinely. "Now you point at it and say *!fooP*. Got that?"

"*!FooP*?" Arthur asked numbly, looking at Cuphandle.

"It's the opposite of *Poof!*" Cuphandle explained, as if Arthur were dim. "You must look at the tree and point when you say it," Cuphandle said patiently as if teaching a slow child. "And put a little body English into it, like you mean it. That was so lame just now."

Arthur felt a bit silly, but he looked at the tree, pointed his finger at it, and said softly, "*!fooP*." Instantly, the tree became once again utterly barren, dormant, and covered with snow and ice. "I'll be darned. So you are a supernatural being?"

"No, not at all," Cuphandle said. "I am a perfectly rational construct of the late alchemical age, about the time when Newton was co-inventing calculus on the one hand in the rational modern world, and on the other hand was making a living by casting horoscopes for a bunch of superstitious fools who, like in all ages, were the people in charge."

"Sort of a foot in each world," Arthur mused. "And two lame ones, at that."

"Well put." Cuphandle pointed to the dash clock. "You only have eleven hours left, so we'd better get zipping and zooming, or you'll miss out on your wish."

The Second Hour

What do I want to wish for more than anything else in the world?" Arthur thought out loud as the truck pulled into his home street.

Cuphandle cranked the steering wheel as the truck turned into Arthur's driveway. "Be careful and think your wish through all the way. You have until the last minute of the twelfth hour to change your mind, and you don't need to commit until then. Take your time and think it over."

As Arthur got out, and Cuphandle climbed out on the other side. Their breath was vapor in the clear, chilly night air. The snow had stopped, and it seemed the entire world was muffled in a thick white coating. A clear black sky was filled with stars, which wavered in the warmth rising from the city. Starlight glittered in myriad fallen crystal facets that lay facing up. The air smelled fresh and invigorating, though breathing it made the rims of Arthur's nostrils tingle with cold. Arthur was glad to be back in his familiar yard with its leaning mailbox and crumbling driveway. High tufts of unkempt, dead grass poked up here and there through a foot of snow.

"Man, what a crumbling pile of brick." Cuphandle stood with his arms akimbo, looking up at the house's narrow, high walls and sharply pitched roof. The twisted brick chimney looked as though a drunken bricklayer had slapped it together. "Is this place haunted?"

"Not if I can keep you outside," Arthur said. He fumbled with his keys, while Cuphandle untied the clock and brought it over. As Arthur opened the door, Cuphandle carried the clock inside. As he entered, all the lights in the house turned on of their own accord. The wall heater in the living room made a whoosh sound as the gas ignited. "Now how did you do that?" Arthur said.

"Tricks of the trade. I'm not going to show you anything more than I already have, and you can't do *Poof!-!fooP* without my help, so don't go getting any ideas."

Arthur shut the door and got comfortable. The djinni (by now he'd accepted the notion that maybe this strange fellow was indeed a djinni) put the clock in just the right spot and sat on the sofa to admire his work. It stood between a wall mirror and a dark table with a marble top. The marble top was the wrong shade of black and white whorls, so he changed the marble to a pleasant marmalade-and-cream that complemented some of the more prominent facets of the very fancy and intricate clock. The clock seemed to tick louder, like a cat purring happily at being stroked. "It likes being where it is," Cuphandle said. "It seems to feel at home here."

"I hope you're not," Arthur said as he shuffled in his slippers to the kitchen. He regarded the old white enamel stove, the tiled sink, and the rest of his anachronistic cookery with familiarity and affection. "Do djinn drink tea? I'm about to make myself some. Would you like a cup?"

Cuphandle sauntered into the kitchen, hands in his pockets. "Wow, ever think of modernizing this place?" Arthur's kitchen glimmered from a single yellowed lamp glowing under a countertop.

"If was good enough for Gretchen, then it's good enough for me," Arthur snapped. "Do you prefer Irish breakfast tea, Indian morning tea, or English high tea?" He pointed to a trio of Victorian glass jars tucked among cracker boxes, grocery bags, spilled egg cartons, and other casualties of poor organization on the tile counter.

"Let me help you," Cuphandle said. He raised both hands and twiddled all ten fingers. Instantly, the counter was bare and clean. The old yellow lamp had become a stylish wall sconce with a red glass shade shaped like a leaping tuna. "Now how about a nice fresh blend directly from a Darjeeling warehouse? Like so." He whistled and pointed, and on the stove sat a popping and rumbling kettle just beginning to boil. As Cuphandle stopped whistling, the kettle picked up in just the same exact pitch.

"You knew how that was going to sound," Arthur said, stepping in close. He eyeballed the kettle and then Cuphandle. "You know the future?"

"In my limited fashion, sometimes."

"So you could tell a man when he's going to check out?"

"You mean—die? Don't wish for that."

"But I could ask for it?"

"You could but to what purpose?" Cuphandle seemed to hesitate. "I'd first have to—*er, um*—check the rules and bylaws rather more closely."

"Oh, so there are limits to what you can do?" Arthur glared at him, licking his lips, with eyes that suddenly radiated lawyers and daggers. Arthur had trashed many an opponent in courts of law. When it came to saving a penny, or preserving Latchloose Bank & Trust, Savings & Loan, What & Not, Arthur was a champion of the inverted yes, the twisted phrase, the fatal noose of well-delivered *aha!*

Cuphandle motioned for the kettle to be silent and the stove to be off. Fresh steaming cups of fragrant tea appeared on the kitchen table, and the two men sat down to drink. Arthur found his tea sweetened just enough to his taste. Cuphandle seemed to prefer tea with milk and honey, just like in Psalms. Along with the tea, a plate of crackers, cheeses, and a little potted meat for dipping appeared. They sat in the quiet, echoing kitchen with its high shadows and mysterious spaces, and were each lost in their own thoughts.

"I wouldn't want to know about the hour of my release from this dungeon of time and pain," Arthur said, thinking of his final hour. "I'd want to have something positive, something useful, something glorious, maybe even fun, but what?"

At that moment, the house filled with a pleasant sound. Arthur jumped a bit in his seat, but relaxed when he realized it was a sound like a gathering wind chime that turned into the repeated bongs of a clock. The sound was fine and distant, but full and perfectly tuned. It came from the wooden chamber inside his new clock. It rang twice.

"There you go," the djinni said. "That's another hour gone by. The hours are going fast, Arthur. You have ten left, after we have spent the first two in idle chatter." He dipped a cracker in artichoke and olive dill dip. "Maybe you are just a complete loser, after all. Or maybe you are just getting warmed up." He snapped out a cell phone and impatiently thrust it against one ear.

"What are you doing?" Arthur asked, rather offended. He sensed that the other was becoming bored.

"I have a date later," said the young djinni. "As soon as this miserable business with you is done, you unhappy and cranky old ugly man, I'm taking a beautiful young *houri* dancing all night atop the London and Paris skylines."

"A young—*what*?"

Cuphandle nodded and smiled at someone over the phone. He put his cell away and said to Arthur: "Not what your miserable little twisted brain thinks. She is not a woman of the streets, but a divinely beautiful creature, sort of like a cross between a sea horse and a Seraphim, or maybe Miss America and a violoncello, but always a dazzling young woman. Nevermind, I can't find the metaphors, the matadors, or the macaws to describe her. Just looking at her would turn you to stone—a forever smiling statue—but that cup is not yours to take in hand just now. You have smaller fry to fish—or is that fish to fry? I still have difficulty with the idiom sometimes."

The Third Hour

S ay," Arthur said, "how come you speak English so well? Aren't you supposed to be from Baghdad or ancient Babylon or someplace?"

Cuphandle made an offhand wave. "Actually, they outsource this kind of work. I actually grew up in a small town in Tennessee. I've worked in the Big Apple so long, that I've picked up the same accent you speak. I no longer ramble in the idiom of Southern colonels and their lost porches and mint juleps. I prefer the neon lights downtown in the big city. I was just promoted, and your sorry case fell into my lap. If I do well, I might be promoted another two whole steps, just because you are so grindingly thick and difficult. I didn't used to have full *Poof!-!fooP* capabilities before this clock gig came along."

"So it cost some Chaldean or Sumerian djinni his job?"

"Oh no, they always promote from within. He's probably a supervisor over a dozen guys like me now."

"And this outfit you work for?"

"That's one of those things I can't talk about."

"Then there are definitely limits." Arthur resisted adding "Aha!"

"Yes, there are limits. For example, you can't wish for more wishes. You can't wish for anything that will harm another person.

That sort of stuff. Seems logical and straightforward, when you think about it."

"Really."

"Mmm." The djinni groaned in satisfaction at his own excellent cuisine.

"Could I bring my wife back to life?"

Cuphandle smiled sadly. "No, Mr. Latchloose, that's on the strictly prohibited list. Also, I can't help you accelerate your path to joining her, if you know what I mean."

"No assisted hara-kiri for me, eh?"

"Not even close." Both men laughed, though a bit sadly.

Arthur, while he thought the tea and snacks were great, had no appetite. He pondered something bigger. "Say, could I ask for immortality?"

Cuphandle shook his head. "Not immortality. You could ask for another life."

"Really?"

"Yes, really."

"Now that sounds pretty appealing." Arthur felt a warm glow inside just thinking about it. "When you're getting old, and your body doesn't quite hold heat as well anymore—particularly during those long, cold nights spent working alone in a drafty old bank office because your wife died on you, and your kids turned their backs on you—the idea of living another life sounds pretty darned decent."

Cuphandle kept right on eating and drinking, with only brief, jerky pauses as this thought or that occurred to him. "Yes, if I were limited in years like your kind, I could see wanting some more time. Then again, everything has its drawbacks. You see, the rules—"

Arthur interrupted: "So, what happens to people when they die?"

Cuphandle stopped and stared at Arthur as if suddenly feeling Arthur was trying to trap him. "I can't answer that unless you want to make it your wish. And the rule book says then I have to kill you, so you'd find out in another second or two anyway." He shook his head.

Arthur shook his head also. "That doesn't sound like a good way to use my one and only wish." He scratched his chin. "So what would the drawbacks be of asking to live a new life?"

Cuphandle thought about it. "You might miss the old one."

"Mister, I'm done with the old one. I've got nothing left to live for except this empty, lonely old house. I don't even have a dog or cat, not even a goldfish or a canary, because, well, I don't know how to take care of living things too well. I forget to feed the fish or the bird, or the dog runs away, or the cat gets run over…that's my luck."

"Would you like to wish for a nice dog that won't run away, or a cat that doesn't get run over?" Cuphandle looked suddenly hopeful, as if this would be an easy case then. He was looking forward, quite obviously, to a rhythmic cha-cha with his houri, or maybe a nice, gliding tango over the skyline under stars and snowflakes. The Eye of London and the Eiffel Tower of Paris looked very romantic and beautiful on a snowy night.

"No," Arthur said, "I want something big and special. I like the idea of a new life. Can I start over from scratch?"

"I'm afraid you have to," Cuphandle said. "Those are the rules."

"Knowing what I know now?"

"Some of it, but not all."

"Like what would I not know?"

"The rules say you can't remember the people who were important in your life."

"You mean, like my wife and kids?"

"I'm afraid so."

Arthur looked at the photos all around. He had them tucked into niches and nooks everywhere, mostly snapshots showing smiling Gretchen and happy children and a rather happy looking Arthur Latchloose himself. "Could I afford to let go of all my memories?" Actually, all of the photos had either been taken by Gretchen, or by him when she posed with the kids and told Arthur to snap them.

Sounding very legalistic, Cuphandle said: "Looking at the upside of every issue, I should inform you that of course you'll meet new people, maybe fall in love again, since you'll start life all over with a blank slate."

"I like that!" Arthur said enthusiastically. "I wouldn't have to put up with my father stropping me and my mother yelling at me when I was small? My father used to come home drunk and couldn't catch me, so he'd beat the dog and beat my mother just to make me cry. And cry I did, all the time!" He did a quick calculation. If he started over, he would buy himself a whole new seventy years or more, starting in a fresh, agile, youthful body at that. "No tricks?"

"No tricks. I'm not a lantern jockey on your lawn, as I already mentioned."

"Let me be legalistic too," Arthur said, banging both index fingers on the table in parallel, as if a binding written contract lay between them. "You're promising that I will have total customer satisfaction."

"Yes."

"That would seem to preclude any nasty tricks."

"Yes."

"No slips of the tongue, verbal banana peels, oratory mishaps, linguistic linguini, or other traps I could fall into?"

"Mr. Latchloose, the only traps we fall into are those we set for ourselves. Now are you sure you are prepared to part with the memory of your loved ones?"

Arthur thought for a moment, rattling and fluttering brief movies of his long-ago family life through a flickering mental projector. "I have to admit, it's a tough one. My wife though, she's been gone a long time, and she'd want me to pick up a new opportunity at happiness. My kids Eddie and Katie had reasonably happy childhoods and they've flown the coop never to look back. That leaves me thinking I should feel free to take you up on your offer."

The djinni spread his hands apart. "There you are." He rose, and once again snapped open his cell phone. He snapped it to his ear. "Excuse me a moment, I have to call this one in. Give me a few moments. I won't eat into your clock time too much." So saying, he strode from the kitchen to seek privacy for his office call, in a large, adjoining bank supply closet. Arthur stayed in the kitchen and had another cracker with potted meat. Moments later, the djinni strode back into. He grinned wide as he put his phone away. "It's a deal, Mr. Latchloose. I suggest we start right away."

Arthur rose and started to take the dishes to the sink. "Do I have to sign papers or anything?"

"No, no, not at all." Cuphandle waved, and the dishes flew away, cleaned themselves, and disappeared into the cupboard. "You signed your contract when you acquired the clock. These are just details."

"Wait a minute," Arthur said. "Do I get to keep the clock when it's all over?"

"Of course. If you play your cards right, you'll live happily ever after, with a nice clock ticking and tocking away in a corner of your new abode."

"I have not decided yet."

"Of course," Cuphandle said, with a new look as if sweat were popping out under his collar. "I suggest we get going. You need time to figure things out. You have until the last minute of the twelfth hour to change your mind. I want you to experiment with your new life and see if you really want to go through with it."

"Okay," Arthur said. "Do we have to go out the front door or something, flap our arms, what?"

"Nothing of the sort. Let's sit in the living room, shall we? How convenient, to live in a bank."

They went and sat in easy chairs near the grandfather clock. "Rather a pleasant room in its day," Cuphandle ventured as he sat a bit stiffly with his hands palms-down on the overstuffed arm rests.

Arthur sat the same way, tapping one hand idly palm-down as if eager to get going to his new adventure. "You have no idea, Cuphandle, how dreary it is to sit here alone, evening after evening, and imagine how it was when Gretchen and the kids and I lived in a nice house in the suburbs. She would come in and say that dinner is ready, or have I checked the kids' homework, or why don't I take the evening off for a change and just stay home."

"It must be painful," Cuphandle said with deep feeling.

"It is. And I'm ready to let go of it all."

"Very well. Let me demonstrate what happens to memory. Do you remember this fellow?"

Arthur stared at the sallow face, with blackish eyes, that conjured in mid-air. It hung over the dully glowing dinner table like a dreadful decapitation with open eyes. "No, I'm afraid not."

"That's surprising. Given how rarely you interact with people, he was a major player in your life just hours ago." Cuphandle pointed his index finger at the apparition, mumbled something, and pointed at Arthur.

Arthur looked again at the sallow death-mask before him and said: "Oh yes, now I remember. That's Major Jarlid. He had to leave suddenly to rejoin his family."

"Says he, says he." Cuphandle waved, and the apparition vanished. "He passed on within an hour after contractually deeding the clock to you. It was the clock that kept him alive, in the deal he made years ago. Major Jarlid, you see, was shot on the battlefield during World War I, when T. E. Lawrence's Arab allies were raiding an Ottoman army garrison near Baghdad. He only made you think you remembered him from your army days."

"You mean, I had never met him before?" This business of magic was beginning to wear on Arthur, since it seemed you couldn't win unless you were a miserable, dead, conniving old soul from long ago, with misery and deceit up your sleeve.

"No, he picked you out of the phone book. He looked under R for Rotten, and then A for Awful, but finally found you under L for Lonely. Had he not been shot, he might have lived to a very ripe old age, nearly a century. Because of his luck in encountering my predecessor and colleague, Major Jarlid was given an entire new life to live, and he chose to start from childhood. Ironically, in one of those twists of fate, he actually did serve with the U.S. Army in Iraq. He got his stories a bit mixed up about how and when he encountered the djinni and the clock. By a supreme irony, he was shot again in the more recent Mesopotamian wars, and recovered in a U.S. Army field hospital before being retired to die in a few years from a ruptured hemo-glow-wormulus."

"I see," Arthur said. "That makes about as much sense as the rest of this prefabricated tale of prevarication and prestidigitation. I'd like to start life over as a healthy, intelligent, handsome twenty year old with a lot of money. Can we skip the baby and growing up phases?"

Cuphandle laughed. "Not so fast, there. I can promise you youth and health to start with, but not material well-being. Skipping the baby and teenage phases will be no problem. You'll know what you need to know so that your wealth in the new life will not be significantly less than what you have here. Why don't we get on with it."

"Okay," Arthur said.

Cuphandle leaned forward with his hands between his knees. "Mr. Latchloose, do you remember the apparition we just saw over the table?" He waved a hand, and a dismal vision of a head with dark eyes hovered in pitch darkness under the ceiling just above eye level. Major Jarlid wore a green saucer cap with scrambled eggs on the bill, and rattled invisible chains in gnarly death-claws.

"Who is that?" Arthur said, staring at the already fading face over the table

"There you go," Cuphandle said. "That's what it's like to replace new time with old time."

The vision faded away completely, and Arthur could not remember why he was staring into the ceiling. "What do you mean?"

"Let's go find out about your future, what's left of it." Cuphandle raised his hand, and nothing happened, but Cuphandle's expression was filled with expectation, as if something enormously important had just transpired.

The Fourth Hour

Arthur sat in the plush chair, looking around. He held his palms against the arm rests, as if holding himself and the chair together. His hands felt clammy, and his heart beat faster. His breath came in short, painful rasps.

"Relax," Cuphandle said, still sitting opposite him. "You're perfectly fine, except that you are scared to death. Well, not quite to death. There's that idiom again. Darn it!"

"I feel this terrible sense that a weight has descended on me."

"That is the weight of terror, Mr. Latchloose. It's nothing to worry about. We're all terrified from time to time, but we only die once, and in that case it's usually over in a second or two."

Arthur saw his pale reflection in the parlor mirror, and gripped the seat with both fists. He said through gritted teeth: "I don't want to feel this way."

"The seconds keep on ticking. See, you are alive. It will go away of its own accord, if you can just relax. Focus your mind on what you have to do now. You have just hours now in which to decide whether or not you wish to live out your old life, or start an entirely new one. I think a new one sounds rather exciting, don't you?" In his eyes danced a vision of a lovely houri in a little black dress and high heels. Her skin was pale as ice. Her long black hair swayed from side to side. She snapped her fingers, and made rumba motions with her rear end. Most importantly, she kept her face averted. Arthur knew, instinctively, that if she ever turned to face him, he would turn to stone. She was to beauty what Medusa was to ugliness. No wonder Cuphandle was so excited and looking forward to his date. Arthur was considerably less wrapped up in his own imagined cleverness, and more impressed with his djinni friend's powers.

Arthur licked his dry lips. In an instant, Cuphandle the djinni made a glass of water appear in his hand, and Arthur drank the fresh liquid. It made his mouth feel less dry, and his throat less raspy. In fact, it seemed to drench his entire being in a kind of calm, cool state. It reminded him of the stillness of a pool in moonlight.

Cuphandle rose and walked to the clock. "Come here, Mr. Latchloose." Arthur rose and stepped beside him. "Reach out and take down the little watch." Arthur looked up at the silvery clock face with its gilded accents. He looked at its complex of tiny, whirring dials and the large, ornate black minute and hour hands. He looked at the steadily ticking red second-sweep, whose hypnotic rhythm drew him in until he was almost frozen. "Reach out," Cuphandle urged. "Don't let anything stop you from your purpose. Push on, Mr. Latchloose. Forge ahead. Take the time piece. It is yours, after all."

"I don't think the clock wants me to take it," Arthur said looking at the clock looming over him, which seemed to cling to its inset timepiece.

"Of course it can't bear to be separated from its heart, which is that ticking trainman's watch. But the clock is your property, your slave as it were, and you have the right to treat your chattels as you wish. Take the watch, Mr. Latchloose."

With trembling fingers, Arthur fumbled about the edges of the watch, until his fingernails caught on a faint ledge there. He dug his nails in and pulled. With a faintly audible sigh or a sucking sound, the vest pocket watch came free. It nearly fell on the ground, and both Arthur and Cuphandle lurched to catch it. Arthur caught it in mid-fall. Instantly, the exotic case-clock tocked more slowly, and almost seemed to droop in the shadows. It was sad, and wanted its heart back, but like the genie, it knew it had a job to do.

Cuphandle said: "Small as it is, it is the master of the larger clock, as the heart is the mistress of life and the master of love. It is also the boss of your time during these twelve hours. See the time on it? It is no longer tracking whatever time it is in the world around us. It is tracking your personal time now."

Arthur noted that it read 3:30, and tucked it safely in to his pants pocket. "How did the time fly by so fast? Where do the hours go? Is there a heaven for bygone hours?"

"There you go," Cuphandle said from across the room, applauding. "You have become the philosopher you need to be." He stopped clapping. "Come, let me show you something."

Arthur followed him from room to room, and Cuphandle did something strange. He lingered here, there, in many places, running a fingertip idly along a counter top, or tracing the edge of a glass-paned, wood-edged cupboard door. "You notice anything?"

"No. Should I?"

"It's not what's there, but what's not there."

"I don't get it."

"Pictures. Photos. Mementos of your past life. They are disappearing one by one. Fading. And along with them, both the happy and painful memories."

"Good riddance to all of it," Arthur said. "I'll make a new start."

"Feeling a twinge of regret?"

"No," Arthur said stubbornly. Then: "Yes," he admitted.

"Seems only natural. You'll get through it."

"I'm not feeling terror anymore, either."

"That's a good sign. Come, I want to take you for a ride. Got your watch?"

"Right here." Arthur patted the warm bulge in his pocket. The thick, heavy metal case felt solid to the touch, and smooth.

They went outside, down the porch, down the walk, and to Cuphandle's truck. Only it wasn't a truck anymore, but a solidly built, handsome dark gray limousine. Cuphandle drove, while Arthur sat in the back seat. It was plush and comfortable. The interior was done in white leather. Its lights glowed under dreamy milk-glass sconces engraved with lilies. The ceiling-seams were studded with tiny tokens of Christmas—red and white striped candy canes, green holly leaves with red berries, and even a few miniature, glossy red and silver ball ornaments. Cuphandle flicked on the radio, and carols played softly. Arthur listened absently for a few minutes while the dark city skyline fled past outside. Every few seconds, at regular intervals, his face would briefly light up under a street lamp and then grow dark again. While a choir hummed in the background, a lady sang Silent Night in a soprano voice as thick and smooth as fine linen. "Turn that off!" Arthur said. "I'm sick of Christmas carols. Haven't listened to any in years, and I hope I never have to again!"

"Of course," Cuphandle said quietly, and the music stopped. Arthur heard only the faint whistle of air outside, the hum of the engine, and the whisper of the car heater. "Recognize this building?" Cuphandle said, pointing to a rather boxy old brick structure that looked like a bank.

Arthur leaned forward as the car crawled to a stop across the street. Arthur stared at the building, thinking it had some significance, but he couldn't remember quite what. "No, I'm afraid I have no idea." It was a rambling old brick structure whose sign had not been lit up for years: Latchloose Broke & Trashed, Inc. Just one little red 'a' in Trashed flickered on and off in a remaining signal of life, oddly in sync with the throbbing of the watch in his pocket.

"The process is working then," Cuphandle said.

"Am I getting younger already?"

"No. That will happen during the stroke of one o'clock at the end the twelfth hour, should you not have changed your mind about this?"

"Why would I change my mind?" Arthur said. "I'm happy to think about being young again and starting over. Already, I hardly remember anything, and the weight of years of sadness is lifting. I'm starting to remember what it feels like to be free."

Cuphandle turned and put a finger over his lips. "Hear that sound?" As Arthur shook his head, Cuphandle lowered the automatic rear window. Arthur felt a wave of cold air come in, and blinked as his hair ruffled and snowy grit struck his cheeks. He heard, clearly, three clappers bonging on their respective bells. It was a labored, clattering sound not as pleasant as the ringing of his new clock, but there was something familiar about the clock tower's slow delivery. Great bells lumbered in their wooden trestles as their booming notes floated through a blinded, frozen sky. "Hear that?" Cuphandle said. "That's the sound of the hour being rung. Look at your watch." Arthur didn't have to look to know that another hour had passed, and he was within seven hours of irrevocably leaving his old life behind.

The window rolled up, and Arthur sat back filled with mixed emotions. Cuphandle drove on for a while. The streets were dark and quiet, but colorful Christmas lights winked here and there. Many doors had dark green pine wreaths on them, and some had lights burning in them to simulate candles. On one corner stood a group of carolers holding candles, and Arthur stared at them as the limo slowly cruised by. "What on earth are they so happy about?" he said softly to nobody in particular. "I am the happiest man on earth, because I get to start life over again with a fresh, blank slate—no worries, no fears, no tragedies or losses."

The limousine pulled up at a brightly lit shopping mall thronged with happy pedestrians carrying packages of all sizes. Arthur rubbed his eyes. "This can't be happening. It's the middle of the night."

Cuphandle looked over his shoulder and grinned. "Time has no meaning in your zone, my friend. This is where you get out. Oh." He fumbled about his pockets as if he'd had an afterthought. He handed Arthur a wad of fresh dollar bills. "There's a grand, on the house. Don't spend it all in one place."

Arthur sat numbly looking at the money, then at Cuphandle, and then out at the bustling shopping scene. The door opened by itself, and Arthur felt a ghostly wave of cold (almost an apparition of Cuphandle, who however remained in the driver's seat, but whose eyes had a strange light in them for a moment) that almost physically pulled him from the car. "Goodbye until we meet again," Cuphandle said. "Good luck, and please, make the decision that's right for you. Customer service is my first and last order of business." The door closed by itself, and a stunned Arthur Latchloose stood forlorn on the curb as the limousine pulled away and vanished among a thousand red taillights dissolving in a mass of snowflakes.

Arthur heard songs and bright laughter behind him, and turned to face the music.

The Fifth Hour

A rthur felt the wad of bills in his pocket, and had a sense of both security and opportunity. A warm wind escaped from inside the huge shopping mall and ruffled his white hair. The place smelled of dollar bills, wrapping paper, fresh leather, happy greeting cards, fast noodles, and pine needles. It was mid-day. The sky had a mother-of-pearl glow as the sun tried to shine through whitish snow-clouds that brooded over the rooftops. *Very pretty*, Arthur thought as he strode forward on strong legs. He was a man who had taken good care of his physical well-being, never smoked, didn't drink much, and walked a lot. He felt elated, for some reason he couldn't quite fathom, as he entered the thronged hall that echoed with voices. At the same time, he kept getting this sneaky feeling that something terrible was about to happen, but it was a dim, around-a-corner sort of sensation that burned in his gut but he couldn't put a name to it. Many shoppers milled about as they hurried on last-minute errands before the holidays. Everyone had forgotten just one more friend or loved one, and rushed to find just the perfect little gift to fit that personality. Arthur scoffed, feeling light, and free from such nuisances.

The mall was filled with aromas of food and coffee, and each store had its unique bouquet of scents—leather, stereos, clothing, all combining in the ambience of shopping. Arthur enjoyed the racket all around him, but didn't stop until he came to a modern imitation diner. There, he spotted a very pretty young woman and a little girl sitting at a table. He waved to them through the window, and they waved back. The woman was pretty, he thought, though he couldn't think of her name, and the little girl was about eight and very cute. He pushed the heavy glass door open and entered. The décor was sort of kitsch 1950s or retro 1970s, with chrome and stainless steel wrapped around Formica counters. The seats were plush, rouge, and plastic. The music was fairly loud, but once you slid into a booth, it became a mute background noise.

He slid into the booth next to the little girl. "Hi," he said. It took him a moment to remember her name: "Katie."

"Hi, Daddy," Katie said, putting an arm around his waist. He hugged the child to him and leaned over to kiss her. She smelled of candy, hot dogs, cola, and throw-up. Her mother was about 35, attractive, and radiating warmth toward him. "Hi, honey," Gretchen said. Her lips came close, but only just grazed his own, so faintly that he wasn't sure they had made contact. And yet he could taste her waxy lipstick.

"Gretchen." Arthur rubbed his eyes with both hands. "Say, this is a bit of a surprise, actually." He couldn't quite believe this, although he wasn't sure why he shouldn't. *Run with it*, he thought, *it probably gets even more weird than this*.

"Why? You think we're ghosts?" she said with that sharp, quicksilver laugh he remembered so well. It could be biting when she was being sarcastic (how could he have forgotten that?) or fun when she was in a good mood.

"If you're ghosts," he said, "then what am I?"

"Time plays tricks on all of us," said Gretchen, buttering a scone. Her eyes grew thoughtful, though her mouth never lost that faintly playing smile of good nature. "We're not ghosts, so much, as maybe this is a thought I had one moment, long ago, maybe after you said something mean to me."

He put his hand over hers. "When was I ever mean to you?" Something inside him hurt.

She lifted the scone with her free hand and bit into it. Mouth full, she said: "You don't mean to be mean. You are just busy all the time. Sometimes I cry in the other room, so I won't bother you, and you never know about it."

Katie looked up from under her wool cap, with her blonde hair hanging down straight. How odd—every detail was right, even a flea bite or something on her neck, and the little birthmark shaped like a micro-butterfly on her wrist. In fact, now that he leaned close to give her ear a playful nibble, he could newly smell on her breath a strawberry milkshake and a grilled cheese with pickle. "Daddy, you never go shopping with us, or eating at the diner. Are you sort of a ghost of yourself, huh?"

He shook his head. "There's a lot of weird stuff going on today. I bought a clock, and I'm supposed to be starting a new life. So why am I here in the middle of my old life?"

Gretchen sipped on her strawberry shake with two straws and shrugged while her eyes blinked as in 'don't-know.' "We're here, Arthur. For years and years, if you want to spend more time with us."

"We love you, Daddy," Katie cried.

"You're just checking out your old life," Katie said, "to see if it's the one you really want." She was twisted her two straws into a pained pretzel. Her feet didn't touch the floor yet, and she was that typical skinny little rail of a girl with stick legs, hyper-active and always in motion.

Arthur looked at Gretchen. "Where does she get this stuff?"

Gretchen shrugged. "Smart for her age, I guess. Must get it from her Daddy."

Arthur felt a tear running down one cheek. He saw his reflection in the stainless steel milkshake mixer cup. He saw an elderly man with jowls and white hair. He was old enough to be this woman's father, and the little girl's grandfather.

Gretchen gave him her standard, perky look. "You're okay," she said. "Whatever you choose, you know I will always love you, and it's okay by me. Get the most out of life."

"I wish you'd been able to stick around," he said. "I've missed you so much."

"Me too." She gave that light shrug again. "If it's any comfort to you, Artie, I'm happy here."

"How can that be?"

"You'll find out one day, but take your time. And don't let any djinn or clocks fool you into making foolish decisions."

"Gretchen ," he said urgently, taking her hands.

She wrapped warm hands around his. "Honey, you were always so smart with legal stuff and money. I always had to buy the children's clothes, send them to school, pick the paint colors and the wallpaper, order a washer and dryer, get the fridge fixed, and all the other things that make a house a home."

"You planted all those tomatoes and cabbages in the garden," he said, squeezing her hands. "I never understood."

"The tomatoes were juicy, weren't they?" She squeezed back.

"They were the best. When you packed my lunches, I'd pick my sandwiches apart, just so I could eat the tomatoes separately."

"You did?" She looked pleased. "You never told me."

"I never told you a lot of things."

"I told her for you," Katie chimed in. "I told her she was beautiful, the tomatoes were good, and her pies were the best."

Gretchen patted his hand. "You'll be okay, Artie. You'll make the right decision about this. But let me ask you, darling. Did you make the right decision when you kept putting Katie down and bad-mouthing the love of her life? I know Tim Woodpond isn't your idea of a successful man. He has to work two jobs just to make ends meet. They have two little kids, did you know that?"

He shook his head. "Honestly, Gretchen, I'm lost without you. I make such dumb decisions. What does this Woodpond fellow do for a living these days?"

Her gaze grew cold, as he had never seen it. The ice in her look was that of a total stranger. "It's bad if you have to ask the dead what your children are doing. Work has been scarce. He is going to night school and working on his college degree to make something of himself, while he works full-time all week as a cook in a little restaurant. He earns very little, but he has a second job on weekends, collecting parking fees at a lot downtown."

Arthur felt as though a light were going on. "As much as I love Katie, I think Tim loves her more. Why didn't I see that, Gretchen? Why didn't I see how important that is? All I saw was this pimply, skinny boy who kept coming around, and Katie would climb out the window to run away and go see movies with him.

The more I was against that lout, the more she was for him, and the more she was for him, the more I was against him." Seeing Gretchen's knowing gaze, her silent show of sarcasm, her coldly twinkling and dramatic blue eyes, he said: "I guess I just answered my own question, huh?"

Gretchen nodded slowly.

"Daddy," Katie said, "will you walk to the park with me so I can go on the swing?"

How many times had he told her he didn't have time?

Gretchen suddenly looked at her wristwatch. At the same time, Arthur could hear a Big Ben going doink-doink in a clock shop nearby. It was a phony little dee-dah-dee sort of midi sound, but it told him that another hour had rung through. As the chime struck six, Gretchen and Katie faded. He tried to reach out and grab his little daughter. "Stop! If Katie's not dead, how can she be in this ghost world with you?" But Gretchen and Katie walked away, hand in hand, without looking back. Katie fell back to look at something on the ground—just a dirty old picture of a pink bunny that people had stepped on—and Gretchen turned. She held out her hand for Katie, who ran to catch up. They faded away into the crowd of thousands of strangers.

Arthur stood staring after them. They ignored him as if he didn't exist. Or as if he were dead to them, rather than the other way around. Sure, if he vanished from their lives, he was the dead one, in this life. And he had not yet begun his new life. He had no warmth or good feelings about it, just a coldness more terrible than that of the grave. So he had no recourse—he let go of it, let go of the pain, and resolved to move on with his new life.

The Sixth Hour

Arthur Latchloose wandered alone through a mall of happy Christmas shoppers. Something heavy pressed on his heart—some sort of recent loss—but he couldn't put his finger on it. Whatever it was, he had forgotten it.

A heavy flow of pedestrian traffic took him along with it. He just kept walking, numbly, until the mall traffic spilled out through wide doors, out onto a sidewalk where cars sat waiting at the curb to pick people up. Arthur didn't see anyone waiting to pick him up, so he pushed his collar up and jammed his hands in his pockets. The cold still got to his ears and hands, but less painfully, as he walked away from the mall. He walked and walked, until he was in a strange neighborhood. The streets got smaller and less important. Commercial zoning gave way to private residences in a fairly poor neighborhood where Arthur began to watch his back as he walked past housing projects and arid playgrounds where broken swing sets hung askance over flooded sand pits.

Oddly, though it had been midday, now it was getting closer to dusk. Pretty soon, Arthur was walking down curving streets with run-down houses, with lots of broken toys on arid lawns, and jacked-up cars without wheels sitting on blocks. As before, he felt some deep force pushing him along, the way the current in a river pushes floating objects out to sea.

In the fading light, he came to a nondescript little green stucco house with a broken lamp over the simple concrete steps leading to a battered brown door. He knocked on the door, and felt it yield. He heard a television commercial blaring out the virtues of buying a set of four tires on sale, wrapped around a sentimental and phony Christmas theme.

"It's unlocked," a man's voice called out. The voice was harsh, almost angry, and certainly impatient.

Arthur stepped into a musty living room that was filled with the soft chatter of an ongoing football game. There he saw a large young man sprawled back on the couch, watching television.

His son Eddie's appearance matched the disheveled look of the house, and Arthur wrinkled his nose at a faint but noticeable concert of bad smells. "Whew," Arthur said, "why don't you open the windows and air this place out?"

"It's my day off, pops. Don't bother me. I work hard all week." The young man turned a haggard and unshaven face toward Arthur. His dark eyes blazed with anger, and he pointed at Arthur with a grimy hand holding a beer can. "Not one minute are you here, and already you are being snooty and critical. Why did you have to come here and bother us?"

Arthur stood in the middle of the room with his hands in his pockets, shocked at the conditions around him. He heard a baby squalling upstairs. A glance up the rickety stairs toward a dimly glowing hallway bulb, and a litter of cheap plastic toys, told him there was a family life going on here, but what kind? "How many children do you and Mary have now?" he asked. Mary was another one—a cheap slut his son had met while working at a fast food joint.

"Two girls. What's it to you?" Eddie wouldn't avert his eyes from a touchdown in progress. He balled his free fist and yelled "Yeah!" He put the beer down and clapped with meaty yellow-brown hands. Arthur could see he'd put on weight, and he didn't remember the grime around those knuckles. The boy looked at him and said: "I moved thousands of miles to get away from you, you miserable old codger. I hate you, you know? You and that blasted bank of yours, and your money."

"I could send you some money," Arthur suggested, "to help out. You're my son, after all."

"Oh you finally figured that out, did you? Took you that long after Mom died? Why start now, after all these years? Don't bother. We've gotten along fine without your money for a long time. No reason to change things now."

Arthur felt sick inside. "Look, I know I was always pushing you, and now I understand things a little better. The more I pushed, the more you pushed me away."

Eddie cracked open another beer, took a big swig, and wiped foam from his lip with a swipe of a sweater-clad arm. His sweater, his jeans, and his shoes all looked as if they had not been cleaned in months.

A mature woman's voice called from upstairs. "Is someone down there, honey, or are you talking to the TV again?" It took Arthur a moment or two to realize it was his daughter-in-law. What were they now, in their early thirties? Was it possible he had lost so much time with them? "Who are you talking with?"

"Just an old bum," the boy said. "It's nobody." He looked at Arthur with a malevolent curl of the lip. Every word that came out cut like a knife. "You wanted me to be like you. You had no use for who I was, or what I wanted to be. You even took my books away, my toys away, and wouldn't let me play with the other kids, for fear that I would turn into just a normal, happy kid. You wanted to create a miserable, money-counting old bank-rat like yourself. You wanted me to be sixty years old by the time I was ten, you miserable old fool. That's why I moved as far away as I could, and why you never hear from me. And I don't want to hear from you, so get out of here and don't ever come back!"

He rose, hefting a sizeable bulge around his waist from lots of beer and fast food. Eddie's very shadow seemed to push Arthur before him toward the door.

Arthur backed away. He felt revulsion and soul-ache as he smelled a blast of beer and chalky breath, not to mention stale sweat and cold motor oil ingrained in the tortured weave of that cheap wool sweater fabric. Edward's greenish-brown teeth spat out more words, and Arthur could only watch his lips move up and down, weaving webs of whitish spittle. "You did everything you could to make me and Mary feel worthless. Mom died because of the way you ignored her, and kept putting all of us down, you miserable worthless old curmudgeon. This isn't much, but it's all we've got, and we are a million times happier than I ever was around you. Get out of my house and don't ever show your rotten old face here again!"

Moments later—an eternity, it seemed—Arthur stood outside in the dark and cold, staring at the closed door. The loud slam of the door, and the rattling of a chain lock and a deadbolt, still echoed around his shocked head. On the door hung a cheap plastic Christmas wreath. In the wreath was a sun-faded silk banner that read "Merry Christmas and Happy New Year," reused year after year. A white plastic candle with a broken bulb hung upside down from it, as did a bit of green electric cord that had been cut, probably by some neighborhood vandal.

"My God, what have I done?" Arthur wailed out loud as he stumbled from the porch and into the strange city he did not know. "How is it possible? Why didn't I see it? Why didn't I know?"

Mercifully, he pushed the dark vision away, and it faded from his memory, leaving again that feeling of freedom and elation at starting all over again.

He wandered blindly along wintry streets and alleys, until he came to a major intersection. There, above a corner drugstore with bright window displays, was a sort of stainless steel Diner Deco entablature that curved around the top on both sides. Embedded in blue and pink neon in the center, over the doors, was a large electronic clock, which now churned out a series of rock 'n roll riffs—seven of them, to be exact. The watch in his pocket seemed to excitedly churn right along.

The Seventh Hour

H ad enough?"

"Huh?" Arthur turned from his contemplation of the rock 'n roll clock and saw a white taxi at the curb. Its sides were dented and spattered with mud.

At the wheel sat Cuphandle, dressed in a slouchy proletarian cap, sweater, dark jacket, and brown corduroy pants. He wore heavy hiking books and looked unshaven. "Get in," he told Arthur.

Arthur climbed into a torn, uncomfortable back seat with cracked black plastic covers. One seat spring, sharp as a fishing hook, seemed to chase his rear end around, no matter how he wriggled and squirmed to escape its vengeful point. "I can't bear anymore."

"You have five hours left in which to make up your mind about whether you want a new life or not."

Arthur pulled his coat lapels up with both hands and held them over his cheeks. He felt freezing cold as the cab pulled away from the curb. He shivered and trembled, thinking of what he had just seen, and he dreaded that there might be worse to come. If his children hated him so, what must Gretchen think of him? Not the happy Gretchen , mother of small kids, but the woman who had to endure the increasing cantankerousness of her husband. "I'm afraid to see anything more."

"Oh but you must," Cuphandle said. He seemed to be the perfect taxi driver, negotiating tough traffic with ease while chatting with his passenger. Arthur had a snapshot glimpse of him under a street light: driving with one hand while keeping an arm draped lazily around the front passenger headrest, head tilted back in an expression that said he was king of the road. "I insist," Cuphandle said. "How else can you make an intelligent decision?"

"I don't want to."

"It's part of the deal, pal."

"Don't make me. Please."

"I see you are not quite so full of yourself any more," said Cuphandle. "You've left yourself no choice. See, all those years, you made decisions that affected yourself at the expense of everyone around you, and you can't escape the results of that, anymore than you'll be able to escape the results of your decision about starting a new life. You still remember who these people were that you just met?"

"Yes." Arthur thought about it. "Barely." It was true—the awful memories were slipping away. "I'm ready to move on," he said. "I want to go through with it."

"Are you sure? Just want to escape? And learn nothing? Will you repeat the same mistakes in your next life?"

"Not if I remember what I learned in this life."

"I don't know how much of that I can guarantee. Not if you start over from scratch."

"I don't want to start over from scratch. I want to be a college student again—twenty years old."

Arthur and the djinni both fell silent amid their ponderings.

After some time, the car pulled into a kind of tunnel. It reminded Arthur of any big-city traffic tunnel going under a river or through a mountain. It had a round, barrel-vaulted roof glittering in white tile under rows of glass-hooded, bluish lights that grew smaller as their perspective converged away into infinity.

The road surface was wet from rain and snow, but gradually seemed to become dry the deeper Cuphandle drove into the tunnel. Oddly, there were no lanes marked on the road, and there was no sign of another car. Not even one. They were driving alone into some sort of abyss.

"Where are you taking me?" Arthur said. He kept his hands in his pockets, shivering with cold, but his face glued to the window in growing apprehension as the road went deeper into the darkness. At least there were still lights overhead. Cuphandle did not immediately answer but kept driving at a steady pace. Arthur could see, in the stabbing headlight beams, that the road surface ahead grew sandy. There still seemed to be asphalt, but increasingly there were drifts of sand laid out in frozen waves, as if a wind sometimes blew through here and then abated. "Where are you taking me?" Arthur asked again, and still Cuphandle did not answer. Soon enough, the sand grew so deep that the car began to slough sideways and lose traction. That was where Cuphandle stopped, put the transmission in Park, and got out. "Here we are."

Arthur climbed out and looked about. Cuphandle walked around the still-running car, whose headlights added light to the wan illumination of the bluish lamps high up under the barrel-vaulted ceiling. "Here you go," Cuphandle said. "This is where your journey really begins."

"What is this place?" Arthur pinched his collar close and stamped his feet. His breath escaped in ragged puffs of vapor, and the cold hurt his nose.

"This is neither heaven, nor hell, nor earth," Cuphandle said. "This is Time itself, or I should say this is one of the infinitely many tunnels through which Time has flowed. Don't worry, it gets a little warmer further in, closer to the Future. That's where you will find your new life, after we make just one or two more stops."

"I can't wait to get going!"

"Well spoken," Cuphandle said. "I have to go back to the Present and do my job." He repeatedly flicked his cell phone open and shut. "And I have an important date."

"The clock," Arthur said, suddenly remembering his house and his kitchen and his bank and his money. Memories came and went like the patchy vapor breath that escaped from his lips. He slapped himself lightly on the temple several times to try and jog his mind. Then he rubbed his nose to keep it warm. "I can't quite remember my life now, except for little particles of this and that."

Cuphandle stood with his hands in his pockets and nodded. "That's how it's supposed to work. You're doing fine, old man. Come on, I'll walk a little way with you."

They walked together down the huge tunnel, which was wide enough to bear eight lanes of traffic, but it grew choked up, a third of the way, with sand growing ever deeper, piled ever higher. Arthur saw lumps and humps in the sand too, as they walked. He began to see tips of things sticking out—a corner of an old car roof, with a bit of windshield glittering in the bluish light. He saw a child's doll sprawled on the sand as if it had floated here on a tide and been deposited by receding water. He saw a wheelbarrow on its head, and a scattering of hard-bound books whose spines were broken, and whose fading pages fluttered crisply in a subway-underground wind smelling of oil and rubber, of water and concrete, as some invisible metro train whined closer and just as abruptly made its ghostly, clattering departure in Doppler time.

Arthur picked up one book that seemed to have a particularly fine leather cover, and flipped through its heavy pages. Its print was in a foreign alphabet, and seemed to fade to sheer white as he looked at it, so he dropped the book. Whatever it had said, it was forgotten even as the words still formed in his reading mind.

They came to a mass of steel that twisted up out of the sand. Upon close inspection, it looked to be a railroad track. Some enormous force had broken several of the ties, but one red signal light still winked on and off on a leaning steel pole further along. Cuphandle and Arthur came to a great black locomotive that sat trapped in sand up to the tops of its wheels. The locomotive leaned sideways and askew, and clearly would never run on its rails again.

Cuphandle shrugged lightly: "Remember, Time only passes any place one time. It never comes by again. It never passes twice. Once it flies past, it doesn't matter what it leaves behind. Just broken objects, abandoned lives, broken loves, lost children that never grow up, nothing but fading wreckage."

"My God," Arthur said, "this entire place is filled with desolation. It looks as if the world was dumped here and abandoned."

Cuphandle stood with his arms akimbo, surveying this domain. "You're sort of right, old fellow. We are in a space between worlds here. Better put, we are in a time between times. Don't try to understand it—our minds can't wrap around it, and we see it all as metaphor anyway. The real construct is many more dimensions deep than you or I need to know about, or can know about. Think of it this way. Time flows in great rivers, always forward, but through infinitely many channels. It never comes the same way twice, but it leaves a huge mass of debris. Ever wonder about those socks you lose, or that key you're sure you had in your pocket, or those pencils that always disappear from the glass on your desk?"

"Not to mention all the pens I lose," Arthur muttered.

"Precisely. Time rips through these tunnels in powerful flood, not of water but of a kind of dust like the arms of a hurricane, and what's left is sand and debris. You may even find a stray skeleton or two. Of course, the people living in time don't know this is going on. They just go shopping or drive home or make dinner or call each other on the phone, and put up with the usual minor chaos and turbulence in their lives, because their entire universe is moving in unison relative to all of its parts. Think of it this way. You're on a planet moving through space faster than a speeding bullet, but you can lie down on a summer meadow and maybe at most you'll see those big puffy white clouds slowly bumbling around in a blue sky."

"I haven't lain in a meadow like that since I was a little kid," Arthur said. "I really missed out in life."

Cuphandle shrugged. "Well sure, so have we all. Too busy to stop and smell the honeysuckle." He clapped Arthur on the shoulder. "Do you really think you'll do better in a second life?"

Arthur shivered. "I think there's no way but up for me."

"Okay then." Cuphandle bent over to pick up a discarded walking stick poking out of a small sand pile. The stick looked worn, but had a nice ivory handle carved in a wolf's head. "Late

Ice Age, I'd say," he said while holding the stick in both hands and turning it to examine it. "Nice workmanship. Aurignacian." He leaned on it. "Feels nice. The owner's been dead about 36,000 years and will never miss it now." He walked briskly across the landscape of sand dunes, toward a portal-like opening overlooking a starry night sky.

Latchloose and Cuphandle walked to the top of a sand dune overlooking a white snowy landscape. The tunnel snaked on to their left. Here, in its side, was an opening about 100 feet high and 200 feet wide, semicircular and without definable edges: the tunnel wall simply stopped at the edges of the portal, and a whole world was visible outside the tunnel.

Cuphandle pointed with his Aurignacian stick. "You could wander out there. There are lots of such world-openings in these tunnels of time. You can go out if you wish, but if you do, remember this. The opening begins to close as soon as you pass through, and within less than an hour you won't be able to get back into the tunnel." He pointed to their left, where the tunnel snaked around a bend and continued. "That's where you need to go, to your new life."

"How will I recognize it?"

"You'll feel it in your heart. Not only that, but it will be daylight there. Don't go into any portal where it's night."

Arthur quavered: "And you're leaving me alone here?"

Cuphandle gave him the walking stick. "I have a canteen of water in the car if you'd like. I think you'll need it."

Arthur followed the djinni, who walked briskly back the way they'd come. The white, dented taxi was a distant speck at the edge of this tidal shore of sand, but the djinni caused their journey to last only about a dozen swirling steps. In a few swift, flashing motions, they were back at the taxi. "Do I have far to go?" Arthur asked.

Cuphandle leaned inside, pulled out a round gray felt-covered canteen with a shoulder strap, and handed it to Arthur. It felt heavy as Arthur accepted it. Cuphandle said: "It's just far enough, and you can make it, but you'd better get started."

"Will we meet again?"

Cuphandle shrugged. "Maybe." He offered his hand, and Arthur shook it. Then he said: "Be off with you now, and good luck." He reached a hand to his opposite shoulder, and made a sweeping motion, so that his hand circled before his chest and stopped behind him. It was a flinging motion, and Arthur—in one blink of the eye—found himself standing back on the sand dune where they'd been together a few minutes earlier. The taxi was a distant speck again, and a tiny figure waved to him. Then he heard the sound of a motor starting up far away, and the taxi turned and vanished into the distance.

Arthur glanced at the world beckoning below. He saw a distant village with a church steeple and smoke coming from several farm houses. The place looked vaguely familiar—almost like—yes! His childhood town in the heart of the country, the little hamlet where he'd lived the hard years of his early existence. Picture perfect as it seemed, he remembered it through the patina of years with a veil of pain. Turning his back on the dark forests with their patches of white snow and prowling wolves, and the cozy looking hamlet on the horizon, he resumed his long trudge down the tunnel. The watch in his pocket seemed to stir.

Behind him, from the church in the valley, he heard the long-ago, tired pealing of a single bell. It struck again, and again, echoing up the dale and into the tunnel onto his back. On the seventh stroke, it fell silent, leaving only a faint echo for a second or two. The eighth hour had begun.

The Eighth Hour

As Arthur trudged with his Aurignacian stick, the tunnel grew dimmer, the sand higher, the lights fewer and smaller. At the same time, the light was less cold blue. The air seemed warmer here. Arthur sweated, and had his coat unbuttoned. The canteen got lighter as he took swigs from it. Its water tasted fresh and cool—a welcome relief from the dusty smell of this place. Dust rimmed his nose, and he occasionally took a swig of water just to wash his mouth out. This reminded him of movie scenes about staggering across the desert looking for some old French Foreign Legion fort, except he was in a tunnel, and this was a desert not of sand, so much, as of time.

He continued to stumble across objects. In one place, he passed a forest of marble tombs. He just saw the tops of the monuments— elaborately carved pyramids, obelisks, eagles on globes, a huge acorn topped by an owl, a marble book larger than Arthur and open to pages of sugar-white hieroglyphics carved in fine relief. More and more markers lost themselves in shadows beyond their own shadows. Arthur overcame his curiosity, remembered the djinni's warnings, and stuck to his forward path. It seemed clear to him that anyone, wandering in time, could easily get lost and never find their way again.

At one place, under an amber lamp in the vault above, a partially buried human skull peered at him from the slope of a dust-drift. Could it be the remains of a wanderer like himself? Was it the skull of someone who'd lost his way here, at this point in the past, the way one lost those stray keys and coins and pens and paperclips?

Arthur's walk was relatively easy in patches where the sand was coarse and gravelly or glassy, but harder in places where the sand was very fine and every step required pulling his feet out amid ankle-deep slogging. His 36,000 year old walking stick came in quite handy, but he was beginning to tire a bit. He almost felt the stick's owner haunting him, asking if the stick felt nice in his hand, if the carved head looked nice enough.

Arthur Latchloose walked past a refrigerator, a desk, a large empty stone flower pot, a statue of an elephant, and countless other objects. A little later, he trudged past a statue resembling the Venus de Milo but carved from worm-eaten wood, and with knot-hole eyes that seemed to track after him so that his spine crawled.

The only sound he heard was the flick-flick-flick of his feet in the sand, and the walking stick, and the occasional moan of a puff of wind over a dune. Other than the rhythmic sounds of his walking and the clock ticking in his pocket, this was a world almost entirely devoid of sound.

Finally, he heard a strange yelping sound, and stopped to look around. He was alone here, walking away from his lost past, toward an unknown future as yet unglimpsed, and only now, for the first time, did he hear the sound of another living being. And what a sound! It seemed a strange, unearthly wailing—until he came over the top of a particularly tall dune and saw a pitiful scenario.

Downhill from him, to the left and off-direction as the tunnel snaked on, was a portal. The opening exposed a cramped and twisted town at night, with lights on in houses and shining out of the windows on to cramped, twisted streets.

Just inside the tunnel entrance, ankle-deep in sand, an middle-aged man in rags stood holding a bottle in a brown paper bag in one hand, and a cane in the other. At his feet cowered a sort of plain brown mutt of a dog, a mix of half a dozen breeds, a medium sized house dog. The animal yelped whenever he raised the cane, and yowled whenever the cane fell against his fur. Luckily the old man reeled too drunkenly, in his tattered clothing, to effect a solid hit against the animal's tawdry hide and protruding ribs.

Arthur felt a tidal wave of pain rising inside of him, almost choking his heart into stopping. "No!" he yelled. "No!" and ran toward the two. The stranger gave the dog another whack or two and then looked in Arthur's direction. He had an unruly shock of thin white hair that stuck out in all directions over his spotted scalp. He had a sharp, liquor-reddened face whose veins throbbed in blue webs on paper-thin skin. His eyes were blue and crazy and filled with rage and contempt.

"Stop it!" Arthur yelled as he ran to interrupt the beating. He tumbled twice, rolling head over heels down a dune, and arrived just as the old man raised the cane to hit him too. At that moment, Arthur tripped and fell flat on his face, almost close enough to smell wine-vomit on the man's shoes. The dog, Arthur could now see from this vantage, was tied down by a frayed leash to a half-buried auto wheel rim, and couldn't run away.

"Get away from here, you crazy loon!" the old man yelled. Down came the stick, and Arthur cried out as he felt the sting up and down his back. He felt a gut-churning terror rise up his spine. Again and again the cane came down, but the dog just managed to squirm half out of the way. Most of the time, the cane hit the sand with a puff of dust. When it connected, even in a glancing blow, the animal yelped and shrieked in fear and pain.

The old man spotted Latchloose. "Whoever you are, you're in for it too!" the old man yelled at Arthur. "You and this blasted mutt!"

"We'll see about that. First," Arthur said, "let's take care of this." He took the half-empty bottle away, wrapped in a twisted bag. The old man grabbed anxiously for his bottle. Arthur threw it as far as he could, and it shattered with a loud, satisfying pop against the tunnel wall. Arthur could hear a pleasing tinkle of broken glass, and an equally satisfying sound of liquor gurgling away lost into the sand.

"No!" the old man cried feebly, as if he'd lost his best friend, or like a small child whose toy had been snatched away. He seemed heartbroken, and angry, but in a stony way that left Arthur chilled.

"So much for your stupid liquor. Next, let's take care of this." He took the cane from the other, who fell to his knees, disarmed and cowering. Arthur waved the cane. "You want some of your own medicine?"

The toothless man wailed helplessly and held his arms over his head. "No! No! Please!"

"I should beat you with this cane and break every miserable, hateful, disgusting bone in your body!" Arthur was beside himself with rage, and it took every bit of restraint not to hit him over the head until the cane was reduced to splinters. "That poor little dog. What has he ever done except love you and try to please you, you monster." He threw the cane as far as he could. Unable to resist his rage, he lifted the Stone Age stick and brought it down so hard on the old man's head that it shattered into dozens of dry, dusty pieces. It was light, and inflicted more shock than hurt. He nudged the old man with his shoe, so that the fellow toppled over and lay in the sand. The man's unfeeling eyes looked up from under bluish, scrawny arms. His eyes were unblinking, in reptilian selfishness and cunning, calculating how to escape or even cause more hurt if possible. *What a hateful old piece of work*, Arthur thought as he freed the dog.

Arthur hugged the whimpering dog to him, and the animal stood gamely in pain and gratitude. "Don't worry, old fellow. I won't let him hurt you anymore." He took the leash off, and the animal limped out of reach, but didn't run away. "Poor old fellow," Arthur said to the dog. "Come along, I won't hurt you. I know where you need to go." He turned to the old man. "You're lucky I don't leave your skeleton here to bleach in this gray light."

"Eh?" the old man whimpered, "eh?"

"You're completely out of your mind, aren't you?"

Arthur stood for a minute looking at the old man. "You have less going on upstairs than this poor dog." At that moment, Arthur was startled to see that a third person had appeared. About 100 feet away, high up on a sand dune, was a boy of about nine. The boy had an eerie, silent look about him, with large eyes deep-set as wells. The dog scampered and limped up the hill and ran in circles around the boy, wagging its tail. The boy leaned to one side and petted the dog. The boy picked up a glass lantern, the kind used in rail yards long ago. An oil wick burned feebly inside, casting an orange light. The boy lifted the lamp high, casting amber light on his pale cheeks. His eyes looked all the more ghostly for it.

"Eddie!" Arthur cried out. "My son!"

The boy stared at him, without uttering a sound.

"Eddie, can't you speak?" Arthur called out.

The boy only held high, and rattled, the lantern so that its glass funnel clattered in its cage.

"You want to guide me." It was a question.

The boy nodded. He pointed toward the village outside, below, under a full moon in an indigo-blue night sky.

"I'll follow you."

The boy scampered down the dune toward the village, and Arthur started after him. Behind, the old drunkard had fallen asleep on the sand. The dog circled around, barking happily for the first time, though it yelped every time it stepped wrong on a twisted paw or bruised bone. The dog sniffed around Arthur's trouser legs and barked urgently, as if telling him he must hurry up and follow. The boy paused once or twice, turning to point his lantern toward Arthur for a second before continuing on. Down they went, out of the tunnel into a windy chilly forest. The full moon illumined their path. Old mossy logs lay fallen here and there, glowing with phosphorescence. Large mushrooms glowed here and there like bone in the bleached light of the moon.

Down they went, into the village, where they walked on gravel paths at first, then cracked asphalt, and finally a neat mosaic of flat paving stones. Arthur felt something familiar about the place, but could not put his finger on its nature. Along the twisting lanes that climbed here and dipped there, most of the windows were dark now, their people gone to sleep. Arthur, the boy, and the dog came then to a muddy yard at the end of a long wall of brown rocks overgrown with wild hedges. Arthur heard the clucking of hens in their roost at night, and the warning clicks from the talons of a rooster on patrol inside the wooden hen house. He heard a plaintive meow and saw a lean, cautious tabby cat hunkered on a wall. Its green eyes were luminous as they followed his every move. The boy went ahead, and the dog with him. The boy lifted a wooden cover, and the dog gladly escaped into the safety of his retreat. The boy briefly fussed over the dog's supper dish and water. Arthur heard the rattle of kibble on metal, the slurping of water, the wolfing of dog food, and a final prostration of gratitude under a last pet on the head, before the boy picked up his lantern and stood pointing to the rear door.

Arthur followed the boy to the house door. He smelled something good cooking, salty, cabbage, with a bit of meat in it, and onions or shallots, in a beef broth. Wandering around after the boy, who certainly seemed at home here, Arthur smelled spices— cinnamon, parsley, rosemary. He smelled other things: rhubarb, strawberries, grapes. They entered a gloomy but warm kitchen. The boy picked up a wooden log and added it to the fire in a rosy shower of sparks. Wood smoke enveloped him, with a sour hint of chimney tar. A door burst open, and an older woman came running in. She had a dark bruise under one eye. Her voice quavered as she spoke the boy's name. Her voice dissolved in sobs as she pawed the boy to her with worn hands. The boy closed his eyes and lost himself in the absolute bliss of her gentle hands that stroked his hair, and lingered on his cheeks, and grabbed his head to shake it gently like a ball. As Arthur watched, the boy threw himself into her skirts, wrapping his arms around her while he felt her tears falling on his neck and forehead. She hugged him to her and rolled him about like a long-lost marble. Arthur heard her wailing there, as she hugged the boy. Arthur stared to let go of the terrible burden he had carried for so long, and almost fell asleep…

Except……except…Arthur's new life was calling from afar.

In his pocket, the watch ticked more fervently, and in the village an old metal bell started slowly pealing, like two chunks of tin clapping tunelessly against each other. It was such a poor bell, in such a poor set of lives, that it couldn't even ring, and there was no echo, just that clapping, clattering sound as if it were falling down a long, hard flight of stairs.

The fire was out, the woman was gone, and Arthur staggered to the door. He felt like a plant torn from its roots, or seaweed pulled up from the ocean. He groaned with the agony of separation. He saw the lantern waving outside. The silent boy stood on a woodpile, one knee up on a log and his slim body angled at rest in side profile as he signaled with the lantern. Arthur knew what that meant. Time to go.

His journey was not over yet. With one look behind him—the door dark and closed as if it had never opened, the fireplace cold and dark as if no fire had burned there in a long time, and the house devoid of warmth and cooking smells—Arthur plunged out the door and ran as fast as he could toward the forest. The boy and his lantern bobbed like a dot of light in the dark woods ahead. Arthur half ran, half crawled and clawed his way up a slippery hill. The snow was real and cold in his reddened, numb fingers. The boy led him to an invisible spot, where he could once more enter the tunnel. The watch in Arthur's pocket seemed to grow excited. The old man still slept in the sand, and there he would lie forever, long dead, in the deepest and darkest caverns of Arthur's memories.

Behind Arthur, a village clocktower rang forth sleepily and tunelessly, one tired clang at a time, a second later the next, until it fell silent on the eighth stroke. The ninth hour was beginning as Arthur stepped through the slightly resistant membrane between time inside and time outside.

The Ninth Hour

Back in the familiar dead air of the tunnel, Arthur found his canteen near where the old man had been. The canteen was nearly empty. Thirstily, Arthur held it over his open mouth and let the last several swigs of fresh water fall into his mouth. He rinsed it about in his mouth and let a few last drops fall on his face. As he rubbed the refreshing water over his tear-reddened eyes, he noticed a light on a sand dune. There stood the boy again, rattling the lantern urgently. His face was an enigma, but his large dark eyes burned with some silent message. Arthur threw the empty canteen aside and slogged up the hill.

As Arthur approached the top, the boy vanished. Arthur stopped and looked around. The sand, from this high vantage point, was still dotted with half-buried objects: a truck with its nose pointed slightly up as if it were a whale breaching the sea surface for air; another truck angled nose-down so that its flat bed looked like another whale's flukes as it dove down. Elsewhere, a painted plaster statue of a Victorian man with mustache and Bowler hat stood beside a pillar on which one elbow rested. Hundreds of multi-colored pieces of paper money from some parlor game lay scattered about. A vase lay on its side. Two broken windows lay in a pile, and a golf club nearby, and a man's checkered pants, and a toy gun…the inventory was incalculable. But no boy, no lantern.

Holding his head with both hands, Arthur staggered down the slope intent on going forward at all costs. He felt a terrible, gaping void in his head. All his memories were gone, or at least the ones that meant something special. He could not remember a single soul he'd loved or who had loved him. He could only hear someone (Cuphandle, whoever that was) saying: "To get new time, you have to let go of the old time. You have to wash the slate clean before you scribble new words and equations on it. To add new, you've got to subtract old. It's simple arithmetic, nothing fancy."

It was dreadful, scary, this stumbling about with Swiss cheese for memory. He seemed to be running down a hall of mirrors set up in the sand. It was like a fun house of crazy mirrors at a beach resort. It was, however, no fun at all. He staggered from one mirror to the next, holding his head. Each time he got to a mirror (or were they windows?) he'd see a scene in there but it would wink out of existence before he could register what it was. That must be his memories being erased. He began to feel a deep, intense panic. It was he himself who was being erased, one panel at a time, like wiping a hard drive clean on a computer. Further down the aisle were a number of shadowy mirrors standing upright in the sand, covered with what looked like drop cloths.

Those must be the system files, so to speak—so he thought. Oh God, no, if I get down there, and they're gone, that will be the end of me. What a terrible mistake this will all have been!

He was on his knees now, unable to go any further. He looked up briefly and saw scenes—a city, a woman, a mall, a girl, a boy, a brick building—fading away to leave only blank chromium-like mirror surface. Simultaneously, he felt those scenes being ripped from his mind like someone tearing paintings out of their picture frames. Holding his head for the pain, he fainted. He pitched face first in the sand. He welcomed oblivion, but oblivion was not quite ready for Arthur.

He awoke groggily as a painful ringing filled his ears. "Oh!" he shouted, twisting this way and that, holding his ears. In a minute, he realized that the pain was radiating from his trouser pocket. He doubled up in a fetal position and struggled to get the watch out of pocket. He fumbled with the knob on top. As soon as he pressed it, the waves of pain went away. The noise in his ears stopped.

Looking up, he saw again the boy standing on a sand dune ahead. Framed by the dark tiles with their occasional dull amber light-lozenge, the boy held the lantern up for Arthur to follow him.

As he rose to his feet, Arthur rubbed his ears to make the lingering pain go away. He realized that the watch had become a kind of metaphoric clocktower—it had just ticked off the final strokes of a now forever bygone ninth hour, wasted in aimless and lost wandering among fun(not)house mirrors—signaling the start of the tenth hour. He had not just wasted an entire life. He had wasted nine hours, and only three remained. He had no idea what he was going to do, or how, or where. And as usual, he was all alone. It was the story of his life. At least, his worthless life since Gretchen had died, and the kids had left him.

The Tenth Hour

With much of his memory gone—and therefore his identity frayed—Arthur stepped from the sandy tunnel, through a portal, and into a dark, smoky metropolis that sprawled before him.

His first glimpse of this unknown place between life and death was an overview from inside the tunnel: rooftops as far as the eye could see; even the horizon was one of rooftops, a skyline etched in thousands of tiny squares of light swimming in a general haze of gloomy light. The next moment, stepping from the tunnel, he was little more than a speck on the city's streets.

It was a hard, dark place. Homeless people wandered the streets. Vagrants gathered at small fires in back alleys to share a bottle and tell tales, while flames flickered orange on their craggy, unwashed faces. Rain dripped off gleaming stone walls. Even the main streets were narrow. Sidewalks were small. Exceedingly tall, narrow houses loomed sinister. No corner offered Arthur a far view, because no street was straight. Darkened shop windows hung on either side. Most shops were closed, and offered very little sign of commerce or prosperity. This world was tawdry, from the gray curtains in people's windows to the battered doors that all seemed to need a fresh coat of paint.

Arthur walked on and on in drizzling rain. He was puzzled. Why had fate or destiny or his lost wanderings cast him up on this triste shore? Was this more about his new life, or more about his old life?

Was he supposed to find or choose a new life? The past fell behind him like an unlit road driven at night. The future lay somewhere ahead, with only an endless gray haze presaging dawn under this drizzling sky. It wasn't so much that the sky was drizzling, as much as Arthur plowed forward through a dripping, damp atmosphere the greenish-white and greenish-gray hues of lead or dull silvery pewter.

With every step he took, he left yet more memories behind. He realized that, in a way, he was now inside those canvas-covered fun-house mirrors he'd seen in those tunnels of time. He encountered only a few souls out in this weather. People were drably dressed, and sheltered under black umbrellas. Their pace was not one of hurrying somewhere but, in this twilight, marked by lassitude, surrender, a depressed slowness as if nothing really mattered.

Just when Arthur stopped out of breath on a street corner, he heard a sort of ragged hoot at his elbow. He glanced in that direction, and saw that a tiny car had pulled up. It was just a little box with four wheels, very much like one of those ancient East German Trabants with plastic sides and a little motorcycle engine. The driver tooted again, and Arthur leaned down to look inside. Through a raindrop-spattered window, he saw a big man in a gray suit: Cuphandle. The driver gestured for him to get in, and Arthur almost gladly pulled open the flimsy door. The inside of the car smelled of machine oil and industrial cloth—the seat covers being partly rubber and forever giving off the odor of the factory where they had been made. "I think you will need a little direction," Cuphandle said. "We are going to sweep together, in one pile, your remaining memories so that you can lawfully and competently decide on your optimum course of action. How is your journey so far?"

"Nightmarish."

"Still want to go through with it?"

"To get rid of some of the memories I have encountered so far—yes. Very much so. But will the future life be any better?"

"You have to decide that for yourself." Cuphandle drove left and right through all sorts of crazy little streets, and Arthur was glad just to be able to sit down in a dry spot. He was tired from hours of walking, not to mention all the emotional turmoil. Cuphandle spied a rare little bistro open and pulled over. "Let's stop for a cup of coffee and a bite to eat, shall we?"

"Yes—I am thirsty and famished."

They ran hunched through the rain and entered a small establishment with a heavy wooden front door secured by metal bars. Inside it was warm and smoky, with a mix of smells of tobacco, coffee, brandy, and a food special somewhere between cabbage and fried sausage.

"You deserve a break," Cuphandle said as they dug into their sausage, bread, potatoes, and cabbage dinners. They washed it all down with small glasses of green, bitter beer. "Not too much of that," Cuphandle said, eyeing the beer. "You must stay lucid."

Arthur pushed his plate aside, wiped his mouth with a linen napkin that smelled vaguely of last week's grease, and said: "How is it possible for me to see my son Eddie as a little boy, a ghost, when I know he has grown up to be a man. He hates me, but that's beside the point. I'm curious."

"Which boy do you mean?"

"Why, the little boy with the lantern."

"That wasn't Eddie. That was you."

Arthur thought about it. That was the craziest thing he'd ever heard, and yet it made sense. The old man, the dog, the woman—they were his family when he'd been a small boy. That had been the miserable life, as an only child, that had shaped the man Arthur Latchloose had become. He saw that scene again, as the woman was torn from him one last time just now: One moment his mother had held him. The next moment, the place had become dark and empty. The fire had gone out, and his mother vanished. All the warmth was gone. Arthur had staggered to the door. He'd felt like a plant torn from its roots, or seaweed pulled up from the ocean. At the memory of that loss, he now groaned once again at the agony of separation. He moaned over the memory of his lost childhood, and how he had already started life anew once before—in the arms of Gretchen, now also torn from him. How could anyone go on? How could anyone start over? There was no going back, either.

Arthur pulled himself together and asked: "What about Katie? I met her in a department store with Gretchen. My wife has passed away years ago, yet Katie grew up to be a woman—who also hates me, but that's also beside the point."

"Ah!" Cuphandle wiped his mouth and sat back, holding his little beer glass in both hands. "I see your question. Well, it's like this. You were asking earlier what happens to people when they die, and I couldn't give you much of a hint then, but I can talk about it now that we're in this phase of the contract. Understand that you will forget this information—whether you decide to forego your wish and go back to being your old self, or whether you opt for an entirely new life. You've heard the expression that, when someone dies young, they're always young and never age? Well, that's about as close as I can come to explaining it. As people grow older, they evolve. They fly through the tunnel along with time, which never passes any point more than once. The old is lost, the new is briefly there, the new becomes the old, and we fly toward the next stage. People become someone new. A teenager is no longer the little boy he was. A young woman is no longer the teenage girl she was. The people we were never come back—lost forever in those tunnels of time, through which you just traveled. Yet they remember themselves as such, if kind of seen through a warped looking glass, filtering out many of the memories. Also, people who loved them, and people who only knew them, remember them as such. In fact, remembering each other is one of the key ways that people understand who they themselves are, or were. In some ways, we never actually die, but stay fixed, frozen, and unchanging in those worlds lost as we grow older."

Arthur interrupted: "But isn't that bad for those who are stuck in something bad? Like me as a boy, in a childhood with an abusive father who is drunk all the time, and beats me, my mother, and the dog on a daily basis?"

Cuphandle made a pained face. "I didn't make the world. I just live in it. I'm just a working djinni like any other stiff—except for the special effects." He brightened. "You did make a bit of a difference back there when you showed the old man what a dreadful fool he was."

"I wanted to kill him."

"But you were restrained about it. How noble of you."

"Don't taunt me about it."

"Easy, Arthur, easy. I'm not taunting you. I'm quite serious. You behaved quite nobly back there. And you were never physically abusive of your family."

"Just emotionally abusive," Arthur said glumly.

"Hmm, yes, you did make a mess of it. At least now you are aware of it. Another thing to consider is that in reality, the boy— you as a small boy—will never experience anything drastically new. Whatever was done to you was done, and that's that. As terrible as your father was, your mother showered love on you. Some good happens to most of us along the way."

"That's true," Arthur said. "We just need to sort it all out."

Cuphandle rose and left a stack of brassy looking coins on the table. Arthur hovered beside him, eager to move on. Cuphandle exchanged *adieus* with the waiter, a short graying man in a long apron, who responded in a foreign pleasantry. Cuphandle told Arthur: "Come on, let's hustle. I have something more to show you."

They got back into the dreadful little car. Cuphandle drove for a good twenty minutes. He seemed to lose his way several times. Arthur felt himself becoming antsy, glancing often at his watch. Sure enough, the watch gave off that aura again. Arthur's gut ached with the sheer raw energy of the clock's hunger for his time. He got it now—this clock not only gave you the time, it fed off your life and your time.

"Here we are," Cuphandle said. "I found it." He pulled over onto the curb, European style.

"What is this place?" Arthur asked.

They sat parked on a small square with a few trees in planters and a row of bicycle parking hoops. Rain dripped relentlessly from a black, swollen sky. Here and there, yellowish light shone from a window—some rectangular, some more like portholes. Occasionally a little car swished past, or a shadowy figure hurried from one doorway to another. The little square was actually more of a triangle, at a fork in the road. A little connecting street crossed between this triangle and the large apartment building adjacent. The building was a bland conglomeration of Modern and Art Deco styles. The houses were surfaced with prickly gray stucco, water-logged with rain. The windows were framed in reddish sandstone, and the corner edges were offset with a few decorative pavers thrown in at random. Overall, the effect was cheerless, efficient, industrial, and unimaginative—not much soul here.

"At last!" Cuphandle said as a door opened. A lozenge of light fell onto the wetly glittering sidewalk. A man and a woman backed down the stairs, lowering a baby perambulator. She wore a pink ski parka, the only bright spot in their clothing which otherwise ranged from dark gray to charcoal. "Take a good look, Arthur."

"Who are they?"

"They are—" Cuphandle frowned. "Something is wrong here. You weren't supposed to see this." He whipped out his cell phone and called the home office.

What was the djinni talking about? Arthur looked at the woman in her ski parka, and the attentive, bland young man in dark clothing who had assisted her. She thanked him, and he responded in kind by raising his hat before hurrying off. She went to great pains to cover the baby with a sort of canvas tent before marching down the street. She looked lonely and unhappy, Arthur thought. Pretty, under that silly rain thing jammed over her curly hair.

"I get it," Cuphandle said, putting his cell phone away. "That was supposed to be a glimpse of you and your future wife in your new life, Arthur." He punched Arthur lightly on the arm. "Instead, it was a glimpse of the past. This young woman was waiting for her husband to come home from work, so they could take their baby for a stroll, but he always chose to work late at night, often accomplishing nothing more than he could have if he'd gone home with the rest of his employees. She had to have a neighbor help lower the perambulator down for a stroll." He looked sphinx-like, saying: "I'm not supposed to tell you this, but those two are about to have an affair."

Arthur stared. "Gretchen didn't do that, no matter how I neglected her." He stared at Cuphandle. "Did she?"

The young man on the sidewalk took off his hat and called out after her: "Gretchen!" Arthur needed no further confirmation of what he dreaded.

The young woman, in one motion, jammed on the brake of the perambulator, and, with an anguished and out-of-control look, fled back into his arms. They stood passionately embracing and kissing as the rain fell around them.

Cuphandle started the car. "Sometimes it works out like that. She had a long affair with him, and loved him deeply, even as she stayed by your side for the kids' sake. She did love you, Arthur. You just did nothing in return but pay the bills on time, which wasn't enough for either the kids or Gretchen. Her young man died two years later in a car accident, and she never got over her grief."

"She never told me a thing," Arthur said, agape.

"How could she? She raised the kids and did the best she could. She never did stray again. Her one extramarital affair was enough for a lifetime, for Gretchen anyway. She realized she'd made a mistake, and she would never again think of repeating it. Grief worked its way around inside of her, letting a door open for the cancer that killed her at all too young an age." Cuphandle backed the car off the curb, and out onto the street, with a rolling bounce as the little engine whined into life. "I'm trying hard to make sure you have all the information you need before you finally decide. We want happy, satisfied customers."

"Can't I just start over with Gretchen? I would do everything a lot differently."

Cuphandle shook his head. "Nope. That's absolutely out of the question. That's forbidden. Bringing the dead back to life is our number one taboo, closely followed by sending the living in any manner over to the world of the dead. That's not a permitted wish. Besides, as I said earlier, there isn't any going back. You wouldn't want to."

"I see." Arthur sat back to mull his remaining options. There didn't seem to be much in the way of choices. He slapped his hands over his eyes, threw his head back, and wailed in frustration. "I wish I had never heard of this clock. Can I just give it to someone else? It would have been so simple if I could have just lived my life out as a lonely old banker. At least I was used to it. There were no surprises—especially unpleasant ones like I keep having now."

"You're on the path of your destiny, and there is no choice but to plunge ahead, take your chances, and do what you must."

"I think I must start my life as soon as possible, before the twelve hours are up, and the opportunity is lost forever." The watch in Arthur's pocket seemed to grow warm as the next hour was about to strike. "You do want to be done with me, and go on your date, don't you?"

"Yes. We're running out of time," Cuphandle said. "Listen."

Nearby, in a gloomy church tower with black rain clouds scudding low through it, bells tolled slowly. The tenth hour had passed, and the eleventh hour was about to begin.

The Eleventh Hour

No more surprises like that please," Arthur said glumly as Cuphandle drove across town. "What a dreary, rainy city this is."

"I'm sure they have a few sunny days now and again. You'd be happy enough here if you let yourself. But you never seem to be happy anywhere, with anyone."

"Not even with myself," Arthur concurred.

Cuphandle's cell phone warbled, and he answered. "Yes? Yes? Oh. Yes. Yes. Okay. No. Yes. Okay. Yes. Goodbye." He put the cell phone away in his inner pocket. "New marching orders," he said to Arthur. "We have one more stop to make before I take you to the point of final choice, and no return."

"I can't wait," Arthur said, pulling into himself, sitting back with his collar up and wishing he could vanish into the seat.

Cuphandle did a U-turn in the middle of a deserted intersection and headed for the opposite side of town. It seemed to Arthur they spent a long time driving on elevated roads, looking down on a glittering river and long stretches of refinery chimneys. Red aircraft warning lights winked atop extremely tall steel towers. Wisps of grayish, desiccated clouds drifted in the chilly wind. Down they came off an aerial exchange and into a part of town that seemed just about as drab as any. After the usual ride through tiny cobblestone quarters, where sewage flowed in the gutters bluish-white like a foul skim milk, Cuphandle pulled over on a little street. He pointed to a brightly lit window a few houses down. "Go on," he said, "I'll go around the corner for a beer. Just come get me when you're done, but don't take more than half an hour. Time is getting critical."

Arthur walked alone down the narrow sidewalk, avoiding puddles. Thick droplets of rain water fell on his head from a broken drain pipe several stories above. As he walked past the window, he could make out dim figures through thick embroidered curtains. He knocked on the door and waited. Presently a young woman opened the door. She was tall and pretty. Wearing a long gray skirt and plain white blouse with a slightly frayed collar, she brightened as she saw him. "Oh, Mr. Latchloose, do come on in." She stepped back and he entered into a warm parlor. Several children played on a hard wooden floor. Shadowy adult shapes sat, talking, in recesses. It was a warm, homey atmosphere. "Pardon me," Arthur said, "I'm afraid I am intruding. Why am I here?"

"Not at all," the young woman said. "We were expecting you. The Agency called." She closed the door and kicked a soggy towel against its baseboard to prevent the cold from seeping in.

"Agency?"

She smiled patiently. "The people who set things up. You know." She gave him a lingering look. "Maybe you don't know. They have djinn that look after things?"

"Oh yes," Arthur said, "I am acquainted with one." He followed her into the living room. He nearly tripped over a set of wooden toy train cars. Everything here was old, and plain, and worn, but it had a kind of homey charm."

"My name is Daniela," the girl said. "May I take your coat?" She made no effort to introduce him to elderly neighbor ladies who had gathered for a bit of gossip, apparently, while babysitting their grandchildren, of which there were quite a few. The ladies seemed very solid and rooted in their corner chairs and just barely acknowledged his presence before putting their gray heads back together for resumed whispering.

"Sure." He shrugged out of one sleeve, then the other, and let her take his scarf too.

"Grandma!" Daniela called as she went to a side room to deposit his coat. "Grandpa is here."

Arthur stood frozen to the spot as Daniela casually pushed open a door—to a rather small, dreary back kitchen, he saw, not unlike his own come to think of it. A somehow clairvoyant elderly neighbor woman said: "Mrs. Latchloose, Mr. Latchloose is here. I think he only has a short amount of time." As in a dream, not everything was easily explainable or logical—maybe, Arthur thought, this is a kind of dream.

Arthur felt his throat constrict. His eyeballs went dry. His knees started knocking together. He had a steady himself by holding onto the rather hard, wavy back of a wooden chair.

A woman appeared in the doorway, wiping her hands in an apron. For a second he didn't recognize her. Then he thought she was Gretchen . Then she wasn't. They stood frozen like that, looking at each other. She was about ten years older than the Gretchen he'd known, and her blonde hair had gone white, except for some yellowish threads in it. Her skin had aged, and there were wrinkles around her eyes and mouth, but she'd aged well, he thought. "Gretchen ?" he whispered.

She seemed to get over her initial bright aura of shock. "Arthur!" she whispered and ran to him. They hugged each other, and he felt the exact old familiar shape of her. He remembered the feel of her shoulder bones, her upper arms, the way the top edges of her shoulders curved softly. He touched the lower back of her neck with his nose, and she smelled exactly as she always had. He felt her arms closing tightly around him. "Arthur, Arthur," she said softly.

"Gretchen." For a few moments they were both overcome with emotion. Daniela guided them to a lace-covered wooden table, and another, younger girl brought them cups of steaming tea. They ignored the tea, however, and sat holding hands and looking into each other's eyes. Arthur was sure his eyes looked, to her, much as her eyes looked to him: overjoyed, surprised, and not a small amount troubled. Unanswered questions hung in the air between them, perhaps unanswerable, perhaps not meant to be answered, and perhaps it didn't matter. "I still love you as always," she told him.

"I have never stopped loving you," he said holding her hands in his. He kissed them. "I have missed you more than I can say. But I messed everything up. The kids hate me, and I'm very much alone."

"I figured as much," she said, looking regretful. "I'm sorry I had to go, but it wasn't my choice."

"It wasn't mine either."

"I know that, dear." It was her turn to grip his hands tightly in her smaller, paler hands—which now had age spots and wrinkles—and she kissed his hands. "I am glad you came to see me."

"So how does all this work?" he asked. "Did you know I was coming?"

She shrugged. She made a silly face. "Well, the Agency has a lot of new people working for them, and they don't always have their act together. They said you might come, and you might not, and so I decided to play it by ear."

"So you live here now?"

"Next door."

"And Daniela?"

"Our granddaughter. Isn't she lovely? And this is Anne-Marie, also our granddaughter," she said, pointing to the younger girl, who was a slightly smaller copy of Daniela, but with more mischievous eyes. Daniela looked demure and embarrassed, turning red, while Anne-Marie boldly reached out to shake hands. "Nice to meet you," Anne-Marie said.

Arthur took both their hands and held them. "By which of our kids?"

"Eddie," she said. "Eddie and Annie."

Arthur remembered the angry young man in the distant, run-down house. Arthur let go the girls' hands. "Honey, that can't be." He tried to remain calm and polite so as not to scare the girls. He felt like bolting from the house and running down the street. Gretchen sensed his emotional state and motioned for the girls to look after the little ones playing on the floor.

"Honey," Arthur said, "it's one thing for me to be sitting here talking with my dead wife's ghost. It's another thing to be holding hands with young ladies that don't exist yet, so to speak. I was at

Eddie's house, and it's a total mess. They just have babies at this point."

"That's just it," she said. "You have to understand—these girls are the ghosts of who those children will become. They are pre-ghosts, you might say."

"I'm lost."

"That's okay, Arthur."

"I have to go in a few minutes."

She smiled at him with a mix of sadness and anticipation. "You always had to go in a hurry."

"This one time, when I don't want to, it's not my choice."

"I'm glad I got to hold you just one last time." She hugged him close and whispered as she kissed his cheek lightly and intimately. "I am the ghost of the Gretchen I would have become if I had lived."

"Funny, I met a much younger you with little Katie earlier today in a mall somewhere. She had milkshakes and grilled cheese sandwiches. And I think she threw up."

Gretchen snickered. "Kids."

"I was holding hands with you, and talking, in the diner. Annie made some kind of a little thing out of straws."

"You mean this?" Gretchen reached behind a pitcher on the table and pulled out a bunny made of drinking straws. It was just an outline of a bunny, made of twisted and frayed straws. The straws were white, with fine green red and blue lines running their length.

"Yes, it was a rabbit or something."

"I taught her how to make those. She was going to give it to you as a present, if you came home long enough to spend an evening with us."

Katie smiled and handed the plastic straws to him. He put the bunny in his pocket.

Arthur heard the *guffaw!* horn of Cuphandle's Trabant outside in the drizzle.

"So," he said, standing up. "I have to go. Will I see you again?"

She shook her head, but took him by the arm and led him to the door. Daniela kicked the towel aside, and the girls all gathered around them. "Bye! Bye!" they all sang out in unison, their voices pleasantly out of tune.

"You have to go," Gretchen said. "You have a big decision to make, and I wish you the best luck, with all my love."

She embraced him tightly. He hugged her warmth to him, lost himself nuzzling in the faint perfumes and soaps in the skin of her neck, closed his eyes and drowned in the silvery well-wishes of his angels.

* * * *

When he opened his eyes, they had all vanished. He was in a bare room without a soul in it beside himself. There were no curtains, no wall paper, no furniture, not even a bare bulb in the ceiling. Gone were the children, the granddaughters, the kids playing on the floor, the old grannies gossiping in corners. Gone was the tea, the smell of cookies, the warmth in the air. In fact gone were the night and the rain, for it was dry and sunny outside.

The door opened, and Cuphandle stuck his head in. "Hurry, Latchloose. We're down to the wire now."

Arthur walked stiffly, like a man who has been in a train wreck. He followed Cuphandle to that ratty little Trabant, and away they drove.

Nearby, a clock played a lovely carillon of several dozen bells, and then a solitary old bell solemnly rang out the hours one by one. At the eleventh ring, the old bell fell silent, and the twelfth hour began. It was the last hour, and it would pass in a great hurry.

The Twelfth Hour

S o," Cuphandle said breezily as they tooled along on a great freeway, "have you decided what you want to do?"

Wind rattled in their hair. The weather was quite balmy and pleasant. It was, actually, springtime. Flowers were in the air, the sidewalks were full of pretty, laughing shopgirls on their lunch hour, and young men in sporty cars kept zipping by, staring, and blowing their horns.

"I'm still thinking about it," Arthur said. "What I want to do."

"You'd better think quickly."

"So what if I just wander on over into my new life?"

"That would be the easiest solution for everyone involved, especially me. Very little paperwork."

"But what if I decide to start over with Gretchen somehow."

Cuphandle looked sickened and shocked. "Oh no. Not possible."

"But if I insist."

"Not a chance."

"Customer satisfaction," Arthur said in a teasing and legalistic tone. *Gotcha.* "I don't believe in making rash decisions, my dear Cuphandle. It was a mistake to let What's His Lid talk me into buying this dashed clock without a proper waiting period and escrow. I won't make that mistake again."

They spent at least twenty minutes, sitting on the concrete edge of a round fountain in a public square, arguing and discussing the merits of this and that. Arthur grew ever more even-handed and cantankerous. Cuphandle, on the other hand, took on a growing expression of sheer terror, like a salesman who has spent six evenings visiting, has met the entire family, has taken everyone out for burgers and shakes, and suddenly realizes that his prospect may be about to sign with a competitor.

"I'm just saying," Arthur said.

"Considering all your options just once more?" Cuphandle said cautiously. He spoke gently, as if he had a nougat for Arthur, and Arthur were a ferocious zoo animal who preferred humans to confections. Indeed, as Cuphandle glanced with horror toward his client, Arthur for just a fleeting moment appeared to be a lion seated next to him, with a huge mane, only a crocodile's long, toothy snout. Cuphandle sweated profusely after a bit. He wanted to get down on one knee and beg Arthur, at any cost, to just take the easy way and go, for the love of Marzipan, and start a new life. Maybe he could promise him a fun new life, not like the old one. He could have a splendid education, a lavish income, a horse, a million-dollar DeTomaso-Mangusta Group 4 GT Classic convertible with ballet shoes to properly drive in it, and an endless string of fashion model girlfriends panting after him. *Anything...* Cuphandle was prepared to sob...*Anything...*

Arthur (the real, normal old fellow, not the croco-lion) said: "I don't think there is much in the way of options. Either I start an entirely new life, or I go back to my old one."

"A miserable existence, is the old one," reinforced Cuphandle with grim salesmanship.

"So show me this new life," Arthur said. He looked at the railway watch. "Seems like I still have twenty minutes at this point."

"Oh God," Cuphandle sobbed, "please make up your mind before I lose mine."

"So tell me," Arthur said, "what would be the upshot for Gretchen if I decided to turn the clock back?"

"No!" Cuphandle shrieked, biting his knuckles.

"Not that I plan to. It all seems so unpleasant to look back. I am just about certain I want to try my luck as a new man with a whole new life full of fresh time."

"Yes!" Cuphandle shrieked, biting his knuckles.

"Let's run through the alternatives once more, just to be sure."

"Eek!" Cuphandle shrieked, biting his knuckles.

"What if I demanded that your Agency furnish me with a new life with Gretchen?"

"No can do," Cuphandle said with steely firmness. "We cannot bring back the dead, and we can't make you dead to join her. I've explained all this to you before. We are going in circles now. All a lot of paperwork," Cuphandle said huffily. "In the end, they'll just turn us down."

Cuphandle sprang up and zig-zagged, agitatedly, across an expansive concrete plaza to his parked car. Arthur walked along at a steady, measured pace. "What if I tell you to stuff your clock up your rear end, and go back to my old life?"

"Difficult, but doable. You could go back to being your sorry, lonely old self. And I hope you'd live to be 105 to pickle and marinate in your misery."

"Now, now—temperamental! This is a big decision for me. What if I figured out a way to have my cake and eat it too?"

"I would tear your request up and throw my cell phone in the river."

They got into the car—Arthur, decorously, Cuphandle throwing himself behind the wheel. He ground the gears and almost stripped the synchromesh while darting out into traffic, just missing several large trucks whose drivers laid down long horn blasts.

Cuphandle drove through a string of lights, which were an intriguing blend of colors—green, orange, and red. More horns blared.

Soon, they drove on an open highway. When the horn noise faded, Arthur said: "Customer service, need I again remind you. Let me guess. There has to be some sort of customer satisfaction survey after this is all done. If I just hold back and don't send mine in for a few weeks, to give me time to think about the scathing answers I'll fill in…"

Cuphandle was shocked beyond words. He stared at Arthur, with his lower lip dangling limply.

Arthur continued: "…Then your wonderful houri will be shaking her seat to a different rumba, or maybe a samba with some jazzy Brazilian genie who's after your job and your girl. And that's before they read my scathing comments. Where will your promotion be then? You'll be back in Tennessee, serving flapjacks to traveling djinn on the night shift."

"You miserable old man. I see now how you drove everyone crazy all around you."

"What say you? Can we negotiate about the options?" He quickly tossed out a few finely tuned alternative proposals that did not involve either a live Gretchen or a dead Arthur, or both, or two in either state.

"Well," said Cuphandle, "it would get passed along to Special Plans and Operations. It would be a complicated matter. It would mean that the person you are, and the persons you have been, would cease to exist. They would never have existed as such, and that would mean undoing a lot of things. For example, Daniela and Anne-Marie would vanish. Maybe a slightly different pair of girls would take their place, or a boy and girl, or two boys, or whatever, with Gretchen 's DNA and the DNA of whoever she'd have married if you had not come along. That little boy with the lantern would vanish."

"Ouch."

"Yes. As my client, however, you require that I inform you that your happiness as such is our paramount concern and should be yours, and therefore you should think of yourself in all of this, and let the chips fall for others as they may." He gave Arthur a look askance. "Isn't that how you've played most of your life out anyway?"

The car entered that long sandy tunnel of time again. Arthur proposed solutions. Cuphandle nodded attentively. Once or twice he even pulled out his cell phone and called his Agency for detailed instructions.

Meanwhile, Arthur sat back and let the miles roll by. This section of tunnel had at least two lanes open and free of sand at all times. There were still objects buried everywhere, from grand pianos and tubas to playground rockets and even a sailboat under full sail.

Arthur looked at his watch while the tunnel lights fleeted past in their tile settings. There was only a short time left to go now.

Cuphandle finished his nth phone call, put the cell in his pocket, and looked intrigued. "They said you should try the vanilla alternative. The simple shot. The whole magilla, from A to Z. You don't have any more time to think it over. There are just a few minutes left, before the Agency invokes the fine points, and kicks in the brute-force default—which means simply taking away your present time, and giving you a whole new set of blank time to start over."

"You forget that I am a successful if curmudgeonly old banker, my young fellow. We always think things through a dozen times before making a decision. The old Russian saying is *Cut once but first measure seven times*."

"No wonder you drive people around you crazy."

"What must be, will be, Cuphandle. Have no fear."

After a 15 minute drive they came to an off-ramp in one of those portals that led from inside the tunnel into a parallel world or Nebenwelt.

Racing to beat the clock, Cuphandle kept the tiny car's gas pedal floored and they zoomed around in a tight arc, down into another snowy landscape. It was a city in winter, but Arthur couldn't read the street signs and directions. He supposed people here spoke a different language. Finally, he realized that the street signs were mirror images plus they were flipped end over end, so that sixes were nines and Ls were sevens, and so forth. They raced down snowy u1eW teertS (Main Street) and then on pv1HL teertS (Third Street) until they came to a bridge, and there they stopped.

On a huge clocktower to the left, a giant clock was a few minutes from tolling the 60th minute of the twelfth hour, and the gig would be up. Arthur, and the world he had known, would cease to exist. By default, a baby would be born somewhere in that alternative time, and a whole new life would begin. Arthur kind of liked the idea. He hoped his new mother would be loving as the old one, and his father would not drink or beat the dog, or leave marks on his wife or chase their son with a cane. Arthur could still feel the deep ache in his hips from the beatings, and feel the sting of that cane on his thighs.

The road was blocked by concrete barriers, and soldiers with assault rifles patrolled the border, but the street continued on into a kind of nebulous Nebenwelt. Or whatever. Cuphandle brought the car to a screeching, sideways halt.

Arthur said: "This place reminds me somewhat of the Houses of Parliament in London, with their great tower and 13-ton Big Ben bell, if we were looking from the Westminster Bridge, catty-corner across the river."

"Indeed," Cuphandle allowed with a little shrug, "though of course it isn't. Be assured, though, that Time reuses its basic templates often, with little twists and variations, in many places and times."

Speaking of rivers, a river flowed under the bridge—a river not of time, but of choppy, frigid water filled with floating ice blocks.

The stone quays and wharves were thickly coated with lines and blobs of snow. Frost and ice rimed ornately winding wrought-iron fences that seemed to abound in this city whose name Arthur did not bother asking because he was intent on his decision.

"Hurry," Cuphandle said, tapping the steering wheel with leather-gloved hands. He looked exasperated. "There's only a few minutes left." He held his cell phone in both hands, as if it were a live hand grenade, and stared at it. "Maybe there's only seconds left."

It began to snow lightly, and then more thickly. The clocktower opposite became obscured with snowflakes. A pall of white clouds descended, lowering visibility to a matter of yards.

Cuphandle tapped him on the shoulder and gestured with his thumb. "Out."

"What."

"I said, out. Let's walk to the edge and you can take a look at your new life. Maybe that will help speed your tortoise-like thinking along."

"Very well." Arthur got out. Cuphandle had an umbrella, and together they huddled under it while pedestrians hurried back and forth. Only Arthur and Cuphandle knew, of course, that a parallel world opened on the other side of the bridge just for Arthur, if he decided to follow through on his wish for a new life. Arthur held his lapels together and pulled his chin in, and even at that the chill wind got into his shirt and made him have goose bumps. Large snowflakes slammed against his skin and melted with icy pinprick pain.

Then, abruptly, they were on the other side. Cuphandle gestured for him to step on a certain spot and then walk straight forward. "You don't need to come back. I beg you. Please—just keep walking and it will all take care of itself. It's not the default. You won't be born anew. You'll already have two nice parents and maybe some nice siblings. You'll be twenty years old in a fresh new body, and you'll be able to easily sprint the mile in under five minutes. You can have all that and sixty more years of new life, all in these few minutes, if only you just decide to let go, and move along. You won't remember a thing, and you'll be forever happy, and so will I."

From the other side, behind him, Arthur heard rumbling in the clocktower as the great bells began to wind up for their twelve o'clock ring. First there was a good thirty seconds of carillon song. Then the first hour tolled. Then the second. In another ten seconds, his old life would be irrevocably lost in favor of a new one.

One…two…

Ten more of these and the game would be up.

"But will it be worth doing?" Arthur said. He stopped, with hands jammed defiantly and uncertainly in his pockets, and regarded Cuphandle. "Do I really want to do this?"

"What else could you possibly do!" Cuphandle said, and gave him a shove. "Go, go, go!"

Three…four…five, boomed the enormous clock.

Cuphandle stayed behind while Arthur walked into a summer meadow filled with flowers. The air was warm and balmy. It smelled of newly mown hay, because farmers in a nearby dell were busy cutting the dry, late-summer grass. Somewhere nearby, cows mooed and sheep leaped about. Birds flew overhead in a clear blue sky. Arthur had to shield his eyes with his hand, and sweat formed on his forehead and got into his eyes as he looked up at the birds.

Six...Seven...

"Well, what do you think?" Cuphandle's voice sounded from in the blizzard.

"Peachy," Arthur said. "I like it. So far so good. Much better than the old one. So far."

"Seconds to go," Cuphandle announced gleefully. Visions of houris and martinis danced in his eyes.

"You'll deserve a promotion when we are done, you and I," Arthur called out.

"I look forward to a long vacation first."

Eight...nine.... Almost finished, for better or for worse.

"And a well deserved one," Arthur said, touching the warm, heavy vest pocket watch in his trousers.

The hypnotic quiet of a summer's day lulled Arthur. He inhaled deeply the scents of new-mown grass and blooming flowers. He listened to birds twittering and crickets chirping. Sheep lowed on a hillside, and their herd dog barked for them to stay in line.

Nearby in a field, while butterflies fluttered and birds twittered happily in an otherwise empty and wonderful day, Arthur noticed a dramatic scene. There stood a chubby boy of about nine, holding a bicycle. "It's mine!" the boy cried angrily.

"Tough noogers," cried a snarling, fierce young boy with a backward baseball cap, who was dressed in gang-style clothing.

He was about two years older, and bigger. The chubby kid was no match. "I see it, I take it. It's mine." He grabbed the bicycle from the weaker boy.

The younger boy cried: "But I worked my paper route all summer for that bike!"

"Tough noogies," the older boy said with a cruel laugh. "Stupid sucker. Take some karate lessons, you loser. Newspaper route my rear end…haw haw haw haw haw…" and so, in a string of haw-haws, the merciless thief pedaled quickly away, while his distraught victim plumped down in one motion and cried his eyes out.

It was all that Arthur needed to know about his new world and his new life. It was no different from the old. He turned and started walking back. As he re-entered the foggy in-between zone, he heard the bell tolling the last hours:

Ten…eleven…

Cuphandle had already left, and stood in the plaza talking happily with his date, the houri whose beauty was terrible and heart-stopping to mortal men, and who would never give their heart away to any genie, but dancing all night was enough to make a djinni want to toss his soul overboard.

"Stop," Arthur yelled. "I don't want to go through with this." He strode back into the blizzard, just as that enormous bell swung around on its creaking coffers and crackling timbers, and boomed out one final hour:

The twelfth bell rang. *Twelve….*

"Stop!" Arthur repeated, as he strode back into the snow. The matter was finished…*Well, almost settled…*

What Happened In The End

Cuphandle stood in the blizzard, a huddled figure at the end of the bridge under his umbrella. He nodded and smiled eagerly after discussing his date tonight in the towers above London, and snapped his cell phone shut.

By law, he must wait until the last hour had tolled and the matter with Arthur Latchloose was finished. Cuphandle stood shivering and clapping his hands together. He stomped his feet to stay warm, while his breath came in vapor puffs.

One by one, the great booming bells rumbled their music through the air.

Cuphandle looked intently toward the spot where the snow appeared to whirl so thickly that the gate into Latchloose's new life was invisible. As he stared into the blind spot, it darkened a bit.

As the last boom growled over the landscape, and the gate to the other world closed, he heard a voice yell "Stop!" and then Arthur Latchloose came striding out. "I don't want to go through with this."

Cuphandle had to sit down on the snow-rimed fountain wall. Was it possible?

"I've changed my mind," Latchloose said.

"Too late!" Cuphandle said. "You said stop after the bell rang its last blow."

"Not true," Arthur said. "I said stop twice. The first time was before the last bell."

"I'll fix your wagon," Cuphandle said through gritted teeth. He yanked out his cell phone, punched in the code for Agency, and had a heated conversation with his boss.

* * * *

Arthur Latchloose waited with patient amusement while the young djinni had a heated conversation and then yelled "Darn!" while clapping his cell phone shut. "Very well, Latchloose, you win. Back we go. Now I have to spend all this time doing a new set of paperwork."

Latchloose clapped him on the shoulder. "Well done, my friend. You'll be promoted over your peers for all these heroic efforts. You fix things up, and I'll write you a glowing report on official Latchloose Savings & Loan stationery."

"I suppose you're right," the djinni grumbled. "Maybe I can stop working for Rose Attar and move on up to the big time. Maybe I can supervise a dozen djinni who have to run around taking care of guys like you. I can live with that."

"Very well then," Arthur said, "so you'll arrange for Plan B?"

"It's already been okayed," the djinni said. "Smart choice on Plan B, by the way."

"Thanks," Arthur said. "I'm rather pleased with my decision also."

They walked back to the car, which already sat nearly buried in snow. Cuphandle said: "You won't need to ride back with me. I've arranged to put you back to your new beginning. Meanwhile, I have to turn this wreck in and collect my frequent driver miles. So long then." They shook hands, and parted company.

Arthur blinked his eyes, then opened them.

* * * *

He sat in his high-backed chair beside the grandfather clock in his living room at home in the suburbs, where he and Gretchen had lived for many years, and raised their two children.

He was no longer alone, but in a room full of people who all laughed and talked at once. In the corner sat a large Christmas tree covered lights, ornaments, and cotton shreds made to look like snow. Lights of all colors glowed around the fireplace. A train set ran around and around under the tree, with several small boys eagerly watching the trains.

"Here, Grandpa," said a pretty young woman of 28. She held a baby in each arm as she came near. That was Katie, his daughter. "Which one do you want to hold, Daniela or Anne-Marie?"

"I'll hold each one in just a minute," Arthur said rising with some effort. "Have a seat here while I attend to one little detail, okay?"

"Sure, Dad." Katie sat down with her two daughters, and Eddie came out from the kitchen bringing a small tray of punch glasses. He looked splendid, a clean-cut young man in a snappy red and green Christmas sweater. "How are you guys doing in here?"

"Just fine," Katie said. "Your dad has to do something to the clock over there."

"I'll just be a minute," Arthur said. He took the watch from his pocket and held it up to the clock. The intense feelings between himself and the clock were fading, but he sensed that it was glad to get its heart back. The watch slipped into its docking pod with a snick and a whirr, and would stay there for as long as Arthur owned it, and then it would harmlessly move on to his children. Some day, centuries down the road, someone might be in trouble and require the services of an eager young djinni. Until then the clock would wait patiently. After all, it had nothing but time..

He thought of Gretchen: I can't wait to be with you, but two years gives me just enough time to enjoy the whole new setup back here. You'll wait for me, won't you?

Back in her little apartment in the gray and drizzly city, where streets were narrow, and houses were small, but hearts were huge, her eyes shone. *You bet I will. What made you think of it, Arthur?*

He thought to her: *I could see that there was no way back and no way forward. So I almost hurt my brain, coming up with a solution that bent all the angles, twisted all the language in this contract I signed, and tripped up the whole Agency and their bumbling djinni. I just kept thinking of you, the boy with the lantern, and finally I hit on the one thing that would change everything.*

What was that, Arthur?

I wished and wished and wished...that my father would never start drinking. They granted me that one wish, and nothing else needed to change.

And here we are.

Here we are. Well almost. I talked them into letting me come to stay with you. They said it would take about two years of

*paperwork and hearings, but they promised I could join you when
my time comes. We'll be together forever.*

She smiled him a lingering kiss (no other way to describe this,
and it lingered in his heart for the rest of his life). As she faded
from his inner vision, Arthur opened his eyes. His entire family
had gathered to sing a Christmas carol by the tree. His son Eddie
had decided to join him as Vice President and heir apparent at the
bank, and Eddie's wife Anne was busy running an accounting
service from home while raising their three boys. Arthur's
daughter Katie was taking college classes to become a doctor, and
raising her two little girls. Tim Woodpond, meanwhile, was doing
a darned good job, though poorly paid, what did that matter
anyway as long as he utterly loved Katie? Arthur had a lot of
friends in town, aside from grateful employees at the bank (which
he had just remodeled at great expense to make it more modern
and comfortable for them from the lowest teller on up). Today, it
seemed like everyone in town was visiting to wish Arthur
Latchloose *an Entirely Merry and Most Happy Christmas.*

John T. Cullen: More Books and Info

John T. Cullen is a novelist, journalist, essayist, and science and history writer living in San Diego, California. He is the author of more than twenty books, and dozens of articles and short stories (fiction and nonfiction).

John T. Cullen's main current web presence (begun 1996) is:

www.johntcullen.com/

He is recognized as an Internet pioneer—the world's sixth digital publisher (Clocktower Books, 1996+). He was for years author of the acclaimed Sharpwriter.com (in 1999 named by Writer's Digest as one of the top 101 resource websites for authors). He was also, for a decade, publisher and editor of Far Sector SFFH—the world's oldest surviving professional web magazine of science fiction, dark fantasy, and horror.

He appeared in a History Channel special as the first person to ever decipher the mysterious ancient Sator Square, an enigma that has puzzled historians and archeologists for centuries. As an Active Member of International Thriller Writers, at the annual convention in New York (ThrillerFest 2009), he was thus the only author present who had ever actually deciphered an ancient inscription of world renown, found all over ancient Roman empire—and lived to tell about it.

Among other historical mysteries he has solved through painstaking, scholarly research and careful, logical deduction, is one of San Diego, California's most fascinating stories: the murder or suicide, at the Hotel del Coronado on a stormy night in 1891, of the Beautiful Stranger (erroneously thought to be Kate Morgan in most versions of the legend), and how she became the famous ghost that haunts the National Landmark hotel to this very day.

He has written over a dozen books of nonfiction and fiction (mystery, thriller, science fiction, horror, historical). He has lived in various countries across North America and Europe, and is conversant in several languages including English, German, and Luxembourgeois. He holds a B.A. in English (University of Connecticut, Storrs), a B.B.A. in Computer Information Systems (National University, San Diego), and an M.S. in Business Administration (Boston University). He served six years in the U.S. Army in Europe during the Cold War. He has lived and traveled extensively in Europe and North America, and is conversant in several languages.

His nonfiction includes **A Walk in Ancient Rome, Revised Second Edition** (Clocktower Books 2011) and **Dead Move: Kate Morgan and the Haunting Mystery of Coronado** (Clocktower Books 2008, scholarly analysis). His dozens of articles on historical and scientific themes have consistently been bestsellers on the lists at Fictionwise for nearly a decade. In particular, his history articles, on topics ranging from the Paris Gun of 1918 to the mysterious Regionary Catalogs of Imperial Rome, have at times occupied more than half the top 25 among Fictionwise Nonfiction/History titles.

He authored the historical thriller **Lethal Journey** (fiction, 2009 Publishers Weekly Fall List), combining the most gripping and entertaining elements of both the legend and his painstaking scholarly analysis of the Kate Morgan mystery of 1890s San Diego.

Most of John T. Cullen's fast-moving thrillers, which span the mainstream and several genres, are pinned on a strong male and a strong female lead, who often find themselves romantically entangled while battling terror and conspiracies.

The author's mainstream fiction includes the panoramic suspense novel **Units**, a spy thriller filled with danger, romance, and action set at the intersection of World War II and the Cold War. The background is based on the true story of Hitler's last submarine, U-234, which sought to bring jet bomber parts and fissionable uranium to Tokyo, so that the Japanese could bring a different outcome to World War II by atom-bombing at least six U.S. cities from Los Angeles to Chicago and more.

The author's political suspense thriller **The Generals of October** is one of the most important and provocative novels of the past decade. The premise: what if things in the USA got so bad that we decided to risk it all on a Second Constitutional Convention? After back to back 'serial recessions,' that's just what happens—with unforeseen consequences that threaten to end the U.S. as we have known her. Young Army officers David Gordon and Victoria 'Tory' Breen must uncover a conspiracy involving the Hotel Generals, and save the nation.

* * * *

John T. Cullen's provocative and thrilling novels also include:

Robinson Crusoe 1,000,000 A.D. (the last human, marooned on Earth near the end of time—is there hope of rescue, or a companion?). An entirely fresh and imaginative new take on Daniel Defoe's 1719 classic, which has never been out of print, and has always been on bestseller lists. The cult classic SF movie *Robinson Crusoe on Mars* (Byron Haskin, Paramount, 1964) proved that this is a versatile premise worthy of modern imaginative film. John T. Cullen's 21st Century departure takes us a million years into the future to the ultimate novel of marooning and fear amid a sense of wonder.

"A Worthy Successor to Robinson Crusoe On Mars — I highly recommend this book. Original, imaginative, and gripping. Great material for a SF movie."
—Media critic John K. Muir.

"Awakening in a cave, Alex Kirk believes that he is the only human living on an utterly changed Earth-until he discovers a bloody footprint in the sand. [Cullen] re-imagines Daniel Defoe's classic tale as a far-future survival adventure...Suitable for large libraries."
—Library Journal

* * * *

This Shoal of Space (classic SF involving a perky young obit writer named Zoë Calla, the men in her life—sinister detective Vic Lara and adventuresome zoo curator Roger Chatfield—and their collective children—in a sleepy California town where alien invaders from 100 million years ago come calling—again);

Monopol City (a woman named Tedda is convicted of a crime she doesn't remember, and is condemned to work on a mysterious board game similar to Monopoly—but to play, you have to descend into an infinitesimal pocket universe where matter is compressed);

Nebula Express (a seemingly routine planetary hop turns into a galactic nightmare for Engineers Ridge and Brenna—with the fate of mankind at stake);

* * * *

The author is completing a multi-volume book entitled **A Walk in Ancient Rome, Revised Second Edition.** The premise has never been done before in all the centuries since the Western Roman Empire. For the first time ever, there is a complete tour, for the lay person, of all 14 Augustan regions in the age of the Antonines (150 CE), without the usual religious and cultural, partisan bias that severely clouds the popular understanding of this important topic.

You visit Rome on her own terms, and understand the city and its people like never before. **A Walk in Ancient Rome** has been acclaimed by academic experts as well as several best-selling authors, who understand the educational and entertainment value of what amounts to a virtual tour.

Professors and authors who have sent praise include **Dr. Harry Turtledove** (Byzantinologist and best-selling fiction author; inventor of the modern Alternate History genre of SF); international film producer and presenter **Simcha Jacobovici** (*The Naked Archeologist*, History Channel); **Dr. Anthony Everitt** (best-selling author of a strategic series of biographies of great Romans from Cicero to Augustus, Hadrian and beyond); **Dr. Rose Mary Sheldon** (Chair of History at Virginia Military Institute; world-renowned expert on Ancient History, including ancient cryptography and secret services); **Dr. Fred Kleiner** (Professor of Art History and Archeology, Boston University); and numerous other experts; **Dr. Greg Aldrete** (Professor of History and Humanistic Studies, University of Wisconsin-Green Bay; and more.

Keep up with John T. Cullen by visiting his website at:

www.johntcullen.com/

www.ingramcontent.com/pod-product-compliance
Lightning Source LLC
Chambersburg PA
CBHW020143180626
46810CB00004B/1708